Petey

BEN MIKAELSEN

HYPERION PAPERBACKS FOR CHILDREN

NEW YORK

BY THE SAME AUTHOR

RESCUE JOSH MAGUIRE

SPARROW HAWK RED

STRANDED

COUNTDOWN

Printed in the United States of America.

First paperback edition 2000.
9 10 8

This book is set in 13-point Palatino.
Designed by Stephanie Bart-Horvath

Library of Congress Cataloging-in-Publication Data
Mikaelsen, Ben, 1952–
Petey / Ben Mikaelsen.
p. cm.
Summary: In 1922 Petey, who has cerebral palsy, is misdiagnosed as an idiot
and institutionalized; sixty years later, still in an institution,
he befriends a boy and shares with him the joy of life.
ISBN 0-7868-1336-9 (paperback)
[1. Cerebral palsy—Fiction. 2. Physically handicapped—Fiction. 3. Old age—Fiction.] I.
Title. PZ7.M5926Pg   1998   [Fic]—dc21   98-10183

Dedicated with love to Clyde Cothern, who became my own "Grandpa Petey."

His life was the inspiration for this book.

They that wait upon the Lord

shall renew their strength.

They shall mount up with wings like ea~~gles~~; pigeons

they shall run and not be weary;

they shall walk and not faint.

— *Isaiah* 40:31

part one

part one

Chapter 1

Spring 1922, Bozeman, Montana

The train's steam whistle sounded urgently as it approached the crossing. Bouncing toward the same intersection at breakneck speed, a faded black Ford Model T spit mud from under creaking fenders as it balked and twisted down a rutted road. Passengers leaned out the train's windows, shouting and whistling as the Model T careened over the track seconds ahead of the rushing locomotive. The train whistle kept up a shrill protest.

Cheering and clapping erupted aboard the rail coach. "The horseless carriage won again!" someone yelled.

The driver of the Model T, Roy Corbin, drove with a vengeance. Next to him, his wife, Sarah Corbin, braced herself as they bounced and swerved toward the train depot. This was no sporting event. She looked instead at the bundled-up child on her lap. This was the reason for their trip.

Sarah Corbin remembered two years earlier when the physician had entered the barren hospital room. A fatherly voice could not mask his cruel words. "Mrs. Corbin, regrettably your child is born with deficiencies."

Sarah gasped, the words gutting her mind. What did he mean, deficiencies? She struggled to understand. "Is he not right?" she pleaded.

The doctor paused. "I'm sorry. Get some rest. We'll talk later."

"Doctor, what do you mean deficiencies?"

"Mrs. Corbin. Please . . . you've been through—"

"I want my baby. He's mine!" Sarah interrupted, bitterly. "I carried him for nine months, now I'm strong enough to hold him. Get my baby . . . now!"

The doctor nodded sadly. "Just one moment."

Soon a nurse in a starched blouse brought in a wrapped bundle and placed it awkwardly in Sarah's arms. My baby, my baby, Sarah thought, cradling the child. She reached weakly and pulled aside the blanket. Her bottom lip quivered. "Oh, no!" she gasped.

The baby's expressionless face looked like a caricature placed on top of the tiny, twisted body. His eyes were little brown orbs, frozen in a hollow gaze. His lips squeezed tightly askew under some hidden tension. A numb and haunted emptiness filled the room. Sarah hugged the bundle, hoping that soon the quietness might disappear along with his twisted appearance.

The nurse waited patiently.

"Please leave us alone," Sarah said, her voice breaking along with her heart.

As the nurse's retreating steps echoed down the hallway, Sarah stared down at her son again. Where were the tiny, round cheeks? The delicate lips? The button nose? Wasn't every baby supposed to be perfect? Sarah fought the sick churning in her stomach as she studied the misshapen features. Her husband, Roy, should have been here. But they had not expected the baby this early. Roy was hauling a load of cattle back from Miles City.

Sarah hugged the baby to her breast and cried silently into the nothingness that surrounded her. She wanted to curl up on her side, in a fetal position, and be a young child again with a mother to hold her, wipe her tears, and kiss away her hurt. But she knew that at thirty-six she was the mother now, and no one could kiss away the doctor's terrible words.

She and Roy had decided to call their third child Petey if he was a boy. Now Sarah tried out the name. "Petey," she cooed. The name tasted strange. "C'mon, Petey," she begged, but the baby's stillness spread throughout the room.

The jolting of the Model T brought other memories. The doctor's diagnosis had held no concession. "Children such as this rarely respond to treatment," he said.

Still, after leaving the hospital, Sarah had not given up hope. In matters such as this, even the words of God became suspect. This was not the dark ages. This was 1922, the age of modern medicine. Every day doctors performed miracles. Couldn't someone perform a miracle on Petey?

A costly trip to a specialist in Butte, however, confirmed the diagnosis. "Mr. and Mrs. Corbin," said the impeccably dressed doctor, standing in his lavish office, "we have here a severe case of feeblemindedness. As an idiot, any rehabilitative efforts would be futile."

"What do you mean, idiot?" Sarah had stammered.

"The child has no capacity whatsoever for even minimal sensory appreciation. My recommendation, however difficult, would be to admit him to an institution that could provide for his care."

Sarah protested, "No! This is my son, my Petey. This isn't the malfunction of some machine. No one is taking Petey away. No one!"

To cement that decision, the Corbins baptized Petey at the old Lutheran church in town. With light pouring through tall stained glass windows, the preacher had ended the service by saying, "They who wait for the Lord shall renew their strength, they shall mount up with wings like eagles, they shall run and not be weary, they shall walk and not faint."

Soon after came months of seizures. Two years of sleepless nights. Two years of feeding, cleaning, and holding Petey. Many townsfolk and neighbors called it wasted effort, but every day Sarah spent herself on the child.

She closed her eyes now in the Model T and leaned her head backward, hearing again the many comments from neighbors. "If I were you, I'd take him to the specialist in Salt Lake." "Do you pray for him each night?" "What tonic did you use for your flu last year?" "Perhaps you lifted too heavy."

Where were these people when night after night she or Roy had sat with Petey, scared his next seizure might be fatal? Many avoided greeting her when she brought Petey to town.

Slowly the medical bills had grown. They had sold everything, including their small ranch, until nothing remained for medicine or visits to the doctors. It hurt watching little eight-year-old Billy and his ten-year-old sister, Cathy, leave for school wearing donated clothes several sizes too large. Would they ever have toys, ice-cream cones, or go to the county fair like other children?

"Why don't you love us like you do Petey?" little Billy blurted one day.

That day a decision was forced on the family. That day was the reason for this trip to Bozeman to give up Petey. Petey was being sent to the Warm Springs Insane Asylum in Warm Springs, Montana.

A washout in the road bounced Petey's head as they pulled into the Northern Pacific train depot, a small brick building on the edge of Bozeman. The vacant expression on Petey's small elfin face grew more distant.

The county health nurse met them there. Her soft sandy hair framed a kind face, but her white starched vest fit like armor over her blue blouse. Sarah had expected someone older.

"Please take good care of him," Sarah pleaded, extending Petey hesitantly—he seemed so much heavier today.

7

"I will," the nurse answered softly, cuddling the unresponsive child. "I will."

Sarah remembered their pastor's words: as important as burying one's dead, so was it necessary to let unfortunates like Petey slip from their lives and memories. Sarah reached out and traced her fingers gently across the odd curves of Petey's bent little body. Then a sob broke through her composure, and Roy led her back to the car.

The county health nurse squirmed to get comfortable on the wooden train seat, worn smooth by years of use. She wiped mucus from the infant's twisted mouth and nose. His swollen and coiled tongue bunched into one cheek. The chore of delivering wards of the state to the insane asylum in Warm Springs was the responsibility of the county sheriff. Whenever the ward was a child, however, the sheriff asked a nurse to handle the transfer. Carrying a deformed baby probably wasn't very sherifflike.

The nurse reached and pulled commitment papers from a large brown envelope in her day bag. Glancing briefly through the evaluation, she saw the obvious described in lengthy and complex statements. Shuffling the papers back together, she noticed the ward's name—Petey Roy Corbin.

"Can I sit beside you?" asked a kindly voice.

The county health nurse looked up to find a tall, stately woman. Judging by her beautiful silver hair, the woman was over sixty. A brown silk blouse matched her long skirt. "Please do," the nurse replied.

The woman breathed a sigh of relief as she settled herself onto the wooden seat.

"Here, let me help you with your bag," the nurse offered. As she reached forward, the baby's blanket fell aside and exposed Petey's distorted expression. Saliva ran freely out the side of his gaping mouth.

"Oh, for heaven's sake!" exclaimed the older lady. She jumped to her feet and grabbed her bag.

"He won't hurt you," assured the nurse.

Still the woman fled down the aisle.

The nurse shook her head as the rail car jolted. She braced her hand against the next seat as the locomotive hissed and ground its way grudgingly away from the depot. Soon the train echoed a rhythmic and endless *click-clack*, *click-clack*. The sound grew louder whenever someone opened one of the wooden doors to pass between cars.

A breeze kicked up, sending dust devils spinning and dancing out across the fields next to the tracks. Pungent smells of sagebrush and an occasional whiff of coal smoke from the locomotive drifted through the open windows. Tucking the blanket tightly around the pitiful infant, the nurse settled in for the long ride. "Life sure threw you a curve ball," she whispered. "It's a good thing you *can't* think!"

Chapter 2

Warm Springs Insane Asylum
Warm Springs, Montana
(receiving hospital)

"Good day, bring the child this way," ordered the middle-aged admitting nurse, her smile strained by the repetitive duty. Her blond hair was wrapped tightly in a bun, and her stout build looked useful for combative patients. She directed the county health nurse down a short hallway into a faded yellow examination room cluttered with an odd assortment of fixtures. Chairs lined the walls. An examination table dominated one end. At the far end crouched a solitary low desk. Two rows of dim lights dangled from the high ceiling on frayed, yard-long cords. Air drifted through a small window, making the lights swing lazily. The sharp, caustic odor of cleaning fluid greeted newcomers rudely.

"Here," said the county health nurse, taking a deep breath as she handed over the commitment papers.

The stocky receiving nurse glanced at the records, then took Petey and laid him roughly on the cold metal examination table. "Is there anything not mentioned in the report?"

"No, except the parents gave him up reluctantly."

"Some do," said the receiving nurse. "I've seen farms and businesses lost, busted marriages, even suicide. And you know what gripes me?"

"What's that?"

"There's always someone thinking the parents should have tried harder."

The county health nurse nodded, glancing at her watch. "I'd better get going. I have to catch the four o'clock Northern Pacific back to Bozeman. I have health exams at the high school tomorrow."

"Well, give my regards to the outside world," said the admitting nurse, removing the tiny garments from the child's tense body. "Won't be needing these anymore," she said as she wiped down the youngster and checked for cuts, rashes, or sores.

"What have we here?" asked an old doctor, entering the room. His wrinkled skin looked a couple of sizes too big for his bony frame.

"A youngster, two years old," the nurse answered. "Petey Roy Corbin, from Bozeman— raised by his parents. I've cleaned him, and he seems well cared for."

"Let's have a peek," said the doctor, bunching his lips as if deciphering a puzzle. "For sure he'll be crib bound." He glanced through the commitment papers and shook his head. "Parents even had him over to the doctors in Butte." He placed his stethoscope to Petey's chest and listened, then raised an eyebrow in surprise. "The child has a strong heartbeat. That's unusual for his kind." The doctor ran his hand through Petey's hair looking for lice and other vermin. Then, tugging on the stiff, branchlike arms and legs, he added, "Spastic."

The nurse nodded.

The doctor picked up his clipboard and jotted down the word *idiot*. "I concur with these evaluations from Butte. I wonder what the parents hoped for—a diagnosis of imbecile?" Sarcasm edged his voice.

"Either way, his lights are out and treatment's the same," the nurse added.

"What treatment?" the doctor mumbled.

Later that day, a young attendant from admissions carried Petey to Infants' Ward, a large, cavernous room with high ceilings. A dozen cribs lined each wall. Dirty white paint blistered from the walls, exposing a gaudy yellow undercoat that contrasted with the bright white uniforms and beds. Each cagelike crib had high metal sides. Empty space near the center of the room formed a play area, but there were very few toys.

The attendant walked down the side aisle, glancing at the deformed young curiosities. One child had no visible forehead, only a hairline that started with his hooded eyebrows. It gave him a cavemanlike appearance. Another child had a head larger than a basketball. Many were like the baby the attendant held in his arms, helpless and passive. Several, however, kicked and yanked viciously at the stout bars on their cribs. Of those allowed in the play area, nearly half sat morosely, like banished souls. Two rolled about on the floor, creating a spectacle of driveling, gyrating bodies. A din of grunts and whimpers mixed with screams, cries, and wails.

The place gave the attendant the creeps, with all the mongoloids, pinheads, hydrocephalics, and other assorted freaks. Quickly, he deposited Petey in a vacant crib at the far end of the ward and hurried out.

Long shadows fell across Petey's twisted little face as the sun settled that first day on Infants' Ward. Immediately, a pattern of monotony captured his existence, a pattern marked by two phases: daybreak and sunset. The metronome of life enveloped Petey with this pattern. In the outside world, life diffused the cadence, but in this place there was no life. The rhythm throbbed, soaking into each patient's psyche: daybreak, sunset, daybreak, sunset, daybreak, sunset. Seasons tempered the pulse, but the pattern remained, repeating over and over and over, numbing even time itself.

With the passage of time, absolute and indifferent changes befell Petey's body. Had years passed like hours, the changes surely would have been noticed. His legs pulled inward like dried roots against his tiny belly. Both arms bent sharply at the elbows and stiffened. With his hands doubled back against his wrists, his fingers became claw-like: little crooked talons with no prey. Petey's head bent farther and farther to the left. His tongue writhed about, snakelike.

And slowly a subtle change crept into Petey's eyes. The little spheres, so long unfocused in space, tilted imperceptibly inward, drawing the world closer and closer. One day they wavered, then converged on the ceiling above the crib. A dim lightbulb drifted out of a hazy fog and for the first time came into focus.

Three years after arriving at Infants' Ward, another event went unnoticed. As Petey was given his weekly bath, the attendant lost her footing. Struggling to lift Petey into the large claw-footed tub, she dropped him headfirst into the water. She grabbed him up. "Are you okay, poor baby?" she fussed, dabbing water from the child's eyes with a towel.

The towel hid Petey's unmistakable smile.

A succession of different nurses and attendants cared for Petey. They found the five-year-old easy to care for. Unable to complain, he spent each day in his crib straining his head, gazing about the room. Nobody could read his thoughts, nor could they see the feelings Petey was developing and wanted so desperately to express. All they could see were his fleeting, flickering smiles. Failing to respond any further, his expressions were still dismissed as the shallow gestures of an idiot.

Chapter 3

In early fall of 1927, a young Mexican man stopped by Warm Springs Insane Asylum in search of work. As a migrant worker, Esteban Garcia had slaved for meager wages in the potato fields of North Dakota and the orange groves of the south. At age sixteen he left his family and struck out on his own. Odd jobs in Chicago, Minneapolis, and Sioux Falls drew him westward. Too small for work in the Butte mines, his determination to escape migrant work finally landed him at Warm Springs.

Waiting for his interview, Esteban glanced

nervously around the waiting room with its tall ceiling and stark walls. It reminded him of the police stations many migrant workers knew all too well. Finally, a huge man with graying hair called Esteban into his office. The man seated himself behind an expansive oak desk and lit up a half-smoked cigar. Esteban sat exposed in a single, wooden chair.

The portly interviewer cleared his throat as he glanced over Esteban's application. "Esteban Martin Garcia, age seventeen," the balding man read from the application. Without raising his head, he scrutinized the slim Mexican over his bifocals.

"*Sí*, I mean, yes," Esteban stammered.

"Why haven't you found work in Butte?"

"Señor, they say I am too small."

"What is it you wish to do here?"

"Anything, señor. I work hard. You will see, I will show you."

The interviewer stood, smiling. He dwarfed the young Mexican boy. "Son, many people think work at this asylum is easy work for good pay. Let me assure you it is neither. The fact is, if you were too small for the mines, you're probably too small to be much use here."

Esteban stared up at the immense man with a pleading look. "For what am I too small, señor?"

"Let me explain. First, we get by here on a budget that couldn't support half our two thousand patients if they were in a community. That means our employees are underpaid, overworked, and seldom given much thanks."

"But I do not want big money, señor," the young man argued. "I want to help people."

"We are not a rehabilitative facility, Esteban. We are strictly a maintenance facility. We do little beyond feeding and cleaning. In the wards, attendants often restrain violent patients or lift bedridden ones for cleaning. Some patients weigh upwards of two hundred pounds. How, Esteban, do you propose to do that?"

Esteban fidgeted with his pant leg. "Señor, everywhere I work I have been small. Big bodies do not work hard if they have small minds." Esteban winced, hoping he had not offended the big man. Pointing at his own head, Esteban continued. "My mind is big and works hard. You will see."

The interviewer laughed. "Determined fellow, aren't you?"

"Sí, señor. Can I work now, please?"

"Tell you what, son. I like your attitude, and I'll give you a try. Do you understand what probation is?"

"Probation." Esteban repeated the word, fearful this was his first test of competency. "I think I know, let's see . . ."

The interviewer smiled. "Probation is a trial period. I'll hire you for two weeks, and then decide if you can stay. Is that clear?"

"Sí, señor! Sí, señor!" Esteban nodded excitedly. And work he did. By spring, Esteban became the favorite of every charge nurse lucky enough to have him on Infants' Ward.

Every day after his shift, Esteban walked around the ward saying good-bye to each child. He always stopped longer at Petey's crib. Leaning on the worn top rail of the crib, Esteban talked to Petey as he would a normal child. Before long Petey's face broke into a smile whenever Esteban approached.

Petey had outgrown Infants' Ward a couple of years before, but remained, even as an eight-year-old, because the ward suited his care better.

One day Esteban nibbled on a Hershey bar as he

visited with Petey. Petey's eyes followed the candy bar. "Do you like candy?" Esteban asked. "Here." He broke off a little piece and placed it in Petey's gaping mouth. Immediately Petey's tongue darted back and forth chasing the tiny chocolate bit in circles. Brown chocolate melted onto his tongue and palate. Petey looked past Esteban, unable to concentrate on more than the melting wonderfulness he pursued in his mouth.

From then on Esteban brought Petey a small piece of chocolate each day when he left. After several months he started questioning Petey before handing him the chocolate bit. "Does Petey want this?" he'd ask. Petey would smile, flopping his two contracted arms and grunting.

One day Esteban asked the charge nurse, "What's wrong with the little Petey boy?"

"He's an idiot," the nurse replied plainly.

"What does that mean?"

"It means he can't think."

Esteban shook his head but said nothing.

Several days later, Esteban approached Petey's crib after work. Holding out a small piece of chocolate, he asked the customary, "Does Petey want this?"

Flopping his arms and gurgling, Petey waited.

"Petey, you tell me, you want this?"

Again Petey flopped his arms, grimacing and grunting.

"Petey, do this," Esteban instructed, nodding his head deliberately.

Once more, Petey flailed his arms, grunting his impatience.

"Petey, do this," Esteban insisted, nodding his head up and down in a yes motion.

Petey skewed his face into a frown and turned his gaze away from Esteban.

"Okay, okay, here, I'll give Petey chocolate." Esteban poked the piece of chocolate into Petey's mouth.

Petey's tongue shoved the chocolate bit out onto the sheet. Esteban retrieved it and placed it once more in Petey's mouth. Again Petey ejected it onto the white sheet, along with stringy brown saliva.

"If Petey doesn't like chocolate, I won't bring any." Esteban turned and walked away. Stopping by the door, he looked back toward Petey. Something bothered him terribly about this child but he didn't know what.

That night, a light from the nurses' station, a glassed-off room at one end of the ward, cast a dim glow across the darkened rows of white cribs. Except for an occasional whimper or cough, the children slept soundly. Down on the south end, in the center crib, one child remained awake. Looking up into the darkness, Petey struggled and fought with his body. Black shadows hid the up and down jerking of his face.

The following day as Esteban left the ward at the end of his shift, he stopped without chocolate to say good-bye to Petey. Before Esteban could speak, Petey grunted and jerked his head up and down in an unmistakable yes.

Esteban stared. "*Madre de Cristo!*" he muttered. "Petey, you wait, I'll get chocolate." Running as fast as he could to the nurses' station, Esteban grabbed a chocolate bar from the concession box. Depositing the usual two cents in the can, he ran back to Petey's crib. "Today, Petey, you get the whole bar," he announced.

Petey grinned as if his face had cracked in half. Grunting and flapping his arms like wings, he jerked his head forward and back, again and again, in a gesture of triumph.

Several weeks later, Esteban brought the charge nurse to Petey's bedside. "I have something to show you," he said.

The nurse watched as the little idiot in bed number six grunted and gestured for chocolate. "Esteban, is this what you brought me here to see?" she asked accusingly. "What you're seeing is merely conditioned behavior. Even idiots can be conditioned with bits of food. Now, if you'll excuse me, I have work to do." She turned and left.

Two sets of eyes watched her as she walked away.

Esteban shook his head. "Petey, you're no idiot!"

That same afternoon, a group of civic leaders from Butte toured the facilities at Warm Springs. Always popular on the tour was a walk through the wards.

"Here, ladies and gentlemen, we have Infants'

Ward," the superintendent recited from habit. "Please feel free to ask questions." The group remained deathly quiet.

Turning at the end of the ward near Petey's crib, a balding man remarked to his colleague in a half whisper, "What a bunch of freaks."

Esteban overheard the remark and flushed with anger. "They are not freaks!" Esteban shouted loudly. "They are poor children!"

The group turned and stared as the two men lowered their heads in embarrassment. The superintendent gave Esteban a severe look. "I'll talk to you later," he said. The group filed from the ward, continuing their tour of the facility, fulfilling their civic duties.

The following day, Esteban failed to show up for work. Each time the charge nurse walked by his crib, Petey grunted and swung his arms wildly. Pleading with his eyes he jerked his head up and down, back and forth. But without Esteban, every subtle gesture that had become Petey's language, his way of touching the world, was once again seen as the movements of an idiot.

Chapter 4

Three years after Esteban disappeared, on a lazy spring day, Petey's numbing rhythm of existence exploded.

"Which one is Petey Corbin?" hollered a mulish-looking attendant, whisking past the nurses' station. He pushed along a wheelchair with reckless abandon. The wicker chair had a stained oak frame with nicks and scratches from years of abuse. Bicycle tires supported the heavy affair.

"Bed number six, far end in the center," the charge nurse called back. She knew they were coming over from the men's main compound today to move young Petey. At eleven years of age, he had long ago outgrown Infants' Ward.

Spinning the chair on one wheel, the attendant cruised along the ward as if shopping for groceries. He wrinkled his nose. Even the lye used for cleaning could not mask the wretched sweetness of body waste.

"Number three, number four, number five," the white-clad man counted aloud, closing on the desired crib. "Number six. Here we go." Turning the wheelchair sideways, he stripped the sheet off Petey. "Oh, geez! What's this?" he exclaimed, looking down at the contracted body lying in front of him. "Hey," he shouted back across the ward, "I can't haul this in a wheelchair."

"What now?" the charge nurse muttered under her breath, pushing back from the desk. "Would you rather carry him?" She headed toward Petey.

"He'll fall out before I get to the men's compound."

"Here," she said. Deftly she swung Petey into the chair and pulled a sheet off his crib. Twisting it like a rope, she pried it under his stiff arms and tied it around the wooden back. "If you have him in this chair often, lay the back down and put pillows under him."

"This *won't* become a habit," muttered the attendant.

Petey's head flopped forward, and the sheet pulled tightly against his chest, hunching his shoulders up on each side of his ears. Unable to lift his neck, Petey stared at his knees and strained wildly to grasp what was happening. The spoke wheels started rotating faster and faster with a loud clatter. The wood floor slats blurred.

Approaching the stairs, the attendant tightened his grip on the handles. Roughly he lowered the wheelchair down two flights of stairs, jolting against each step. Petey winced each time his head bounced. Before Petey fully recovered from the jarring descent, the attendant pushed him outside, bouncing hard over the door threshold.

A light breeze greeted them with the smell of fresh cut grass, lilacs, and honeysuckle. The smells could almost be tasted. Releasing each breath reluctantly, Petey quickly gulped more. He'd felt the wind before, but only for brief moments as he passed an open window going to his weekly bath. Not since the day Petey had arrived at Warm Springs nine years ago had he been outside. Now shivers rushed over him. The air flowed across his entire body, tugging at the white sheet covering his legs. It tickled. The sun, long limited to poking only thin beams of light into the ward, bathed the whole world. Even with his head forced forward, Petey squinted and blinked against the dazzling brightness. He smiled, and his eyes watered.

For ten minutes they wound down the long walkway—there seemed to be no limit to distance or space. They rolled and rolled, never stopping. How far could a person go without coming to a wall? Suddenly, a loud beep caused Petey to jerk. A big black contraption rattled past, smoke and dust billowing from behind. Twisting his gaze sideways away from his knees, Petey could see a person sitting in the contraption. He followed its progress as far as his eyes could allow. Blinking in amazement, he grinned, arms flopping wildly. He felt so alive.

"Look at that, kid, it's a new Packard Sedan. Ain't she a beauty?" the attendant commented.

Petey failed to understand what he meant.

"In this new ward you're gonna meet some real stooges, kid." The attendant's sarcasm flowed thick as if leading a tour group. "We got blacksmiths, boilermakers, gamblers, doctors, prizefighters, even preachers, all under one roof. Yup, this is quite the cultural affair."

The walk from Infants' Ward passed all too quickly. A big, red brick building loomed sideways into Petey's sight. The glory of being outside faded quickly. After backing through the front door, the attendant jarred and jolted the wheelchair back up two flights of stairs. Each bump knocked away chunks of Petey's enchantment.

A corner bed had been readied. With a grunt of relief, the attendant dumped Petey roughly on the bed. "Glad we don't do this every day, kid."

Petey eyed the attendant quizzically. For Petey, the trip had been wonderful. Propped against a pillow with his head tilted toward the open room, Petey examined his roommates for the first time. There must have been nearly fifty men, all adults.

Nearby, a tall man with no pants and knotty joints stood on a bed shouting, "Repent and you shall be saved. The day of the Lord is at hand. You are sinners, but I have come to deliver you. Everybody pray with me." The man closed his eyes as if the whole room had followed his bidding. Rocking on the bed, unsteady in his self-imposed darkness, the frail man prayed a prayer worn dull by repetition. He stole peeks to steady himself and to check on his imaginary congregation.

Petey looked beyond the preacher. Near the window, a gaunt man chewed on his half-devoured shirt. His eyes were as hollow as his ribs.

Dozens of patients were scattered about the room, their half-dressed bodies huddled against walls and beds. Most clung to their knees. Some gazed into nothingness or sat on chairs, heads drooped forward, totally unaware of the madhouse or even the flies crawling across their necks. Several stared out the dirty windows, their gaze focused a million miles away from Ward 18 of the men's main compound. In the dayroom at the far end of the ward, half a dozen patients sat around two large wooden tables playing cards or rolling cigarettes.

Noise echoed from everywhere and nowhere. One young man with baggy pants drawn tight at the waist paced back and forth talking earnestly to himself. As if on cue, several patients turned and wandered toward Petey. Curious about the new arrival, they converged as a horde on the helpless sixty-pound boy. Their questions blazed out like cannon fire.

"What's your name?"

"Do you smoke?"

"Did you have an accident?"

"Hi, I'm Joe, I know the President."

A few reached out to touch or pinch the new stranger. Petey looked up at the circle of faces with terror in his eyes. Grimacing, he flailed his arms, hitting the spectators and scattering them like chickens. They stood just beyond Petey's reach, hazarding their remarks.

"You hit me, you jerk!"

"I'm gonna tell Bob."

"What ya do that for?"

"You're gonna get in trouble."

"I'm Joe, I know the President."

Petey cowered until the group moved away. Why had they brought him to this terrible place?

* * *

The first night, Petey whimpered and twitched in a fitful sleep. He dreamed of faces circling his bed. Not until dawn did he fall into a peaceful slumber and dream of his walk outside. He felt the wind and smelled the air. He dreamed of happy voices and of loving arms that held him in a place too wonderful to be real. When morning came, Petey awoke slowly, reality diluting his thoughts into vague shadows that retreated from his mind.

Suddenly the lights flashed on. "Everybody up and at 'em! Come on, Johnny, Sam, Joe! Let's go, it's six o'clock!" An attendant barked his commands as he walked down the aisle clapping his hands and kicking the beds of delinquent sleepers. He went directly over and started cleaning Petey. "This sure is gonna be fun every day," he grumbled, hoisting Petey into the wooden wheelchair. "I have fifty other morons to care for, and the head nurse says she wants you taken out of bed each day."

Petey rested awkwardly on two pillows. Except for a shirt and a white sheet over his chest, the attendant left Petey naked. Petey gestured wildly for his wheelchair to be moved nearer to the window.

"Settle down, dang it!" the attendant scolded. "You'll get everybody worked up."

Petey quieted but kept pleading with his eyes until the attendant walked away. Helplessly, he returned to the unrelenting rhythm of boredom.

If the pattern had numbed Petey's mind at Infants' Ward, here it throbbed even stronger, crippling and paralyzing his existence. Every patient, active or passive, lived with the general din of mayhem that surrounded them. It went unnoticed like the roar of a waterfall as time passed—daybreak, sunset, daybreak, sunset.

Above Petey's bed a large, square heater hung from the high ceiling. In colder months, the furnace billowed with a roar that exacted many sleepless nights. While burning, it cast a dancing reflection of light across the wall and onto Petey's wheelchair parked beside his bed. The heater, not sufficient for the whole ward, heated excessively directly below the vents. Many nights Petey squirmed and twisted, shoving aside suffocating blankets, only to have the furnace shut down. Soon the air cooled, leaving him shivering without covers.

Attendants served food in the dayroom. Unable to feed himself, most of Petey's contact with others came during mealtime. Lying on his back, he often choked on food. Everyone ignored him, blaming it on his spastic nature. Petey strained once to raise his head so he would not gag.

"Hey, fellow, settle down or we'll skip supper," the attendant cautioned.

After one missed meal, Petey resigned himself to the choking. Because of the gagging, many mouthfuls of bread, potatoes, and meat loaf ended up all over Petey's wheelchair. Always rushed, the attendants often forgot to shake away crumbs or small chunks of food which fell in the folds of the sheet covering. Petey noticed the small droppings, but had no way of knowing they would soon bring great joy and one day even greater sorrow.

Chapter 5

One cold night in Men's Ward, Petey lay awake. As the furnace roared, he strained to look sideways at the dim reflection on his wheelchair. Something had moved. He'd seen something move. Squirming and twisting, Petey struggled to see directly.

Again something moved, but as Petey searched the dim reaches of the glow, the heater kicked off and left the room in still darkness. Now Petey heard something: a faint scratching sound on the sheet covering his wheelchair. He stared into the black nothingness, afraid but excited. Five minutes he waited, his heart pounding.

With a click and roar, the furnace billowed back to life, flickering dim light back across the wheelchair. Petey jerked wildly in a triggered reaction. Three little fuzzy creatures scattered, but not before being identified. Mice!

At Infants' Ward, Petey had seen mice and heard the nurses and aides talk about them, but never this close. They were tiny but scurried about so fast. Soon the mice ventured back onto the wheelchair. Unconcerned about the roaring furnace ten feet above them, they sniffed and poked their little whiskered noses into every fold of the sheet, searching for tidbits of food.

For several hours Petey watched the three mice. The large one with the huge elephant ears he named William, the name of an attendant he remembered from Infants' Ward. The two smaller mice could have been brother and sister. One gray, the other black, they became Cloud and Blackie.

After the first few nights, Petey hoped for cold weather so he could watch his little friends by furnace light. He also started guarding pieces of food which fell on his sheet at mealtime. Flopping his arms, he caused crumbs and chunks to settle between the folds, hiding them from the attendant. If the day's food storage had not gone well because an attendant brushed off his sheets, Petey mysteriously broke into a coughing spell, spewing food all over his cover sheet. It became a delicate art. If he coughed too hard, they exchanged his sheet with a clean one.

By mid-November the furnace kicked on regularly, allowing Petey to watch his tiny fuzzy friends every night. Two more mice joined the nightly gathering. One fat gray mouse he called Sally. Another gray one with huge whiskers endeared himself to Petey from the very start. After eating, the mouse crossed over from the wheelchair and curled against Petey's warm body. Eventually he spent whole nights. Petey named him Esteban.

A week passed before a new gray mouse with dark patches showed up on the wheelchair. Reluctant and scared, he fled every time the furnace kicked in. Petey named him Patches. Within a few days Patches became a regular.

Petey grew concerned for Sally. She had grown fat and clumsy. Finally one night she failed to appear. Late into the night Petey lay awake. He watched the other mice. Patches kept running from one bit of food to the next, satisfying his curiosity more than his hunger. As usual, Esteban had crossed over to the bed and curled up near Petey's side, asleep. What could have happened to Sally?

The following night, Sally climbed slowly up the wheel an hour after the rest started feeding. Petey smiled broadly. Sally! She was okay! She didn't look as bloated but appeared weak. She fed determinedly for a short while and then scurried away. Her actions puzzled Petey.

For several weeks Sally only came for short visits. One night Petey heard an odd frenzy of faint squeaks. When the furnace finally kicked on, the light exposed Sally, complete with her litter of five tiny babies.

Sally climbed deftly up the wheel, leaving the little mice crying and bumping into each other, trying to follow. One wheel had quite a bit of rough tread left; the other was worn smooth. Petey watched the baby mice work to climb the smooth tire their mother had clambered up so easily. They clawed their way up a few inches, then fell. If one made progress, another crawled up behind and grabbed its tail, sending both tumbling to the floor. Meanwhile Sally nibbled away, unconcerned.

The smallest of the five babies never had a chance. Shoved aside and crowded out, the runt finally wandered across the open floor to the other tire and clawed his way successfully up the treaded wheel. By the time he reached the top, the other babies discovered the secret and ran over to follow. Petey watched, grinning as the teeny rascals scrambled about. He had more friends!

As winter settled, hard, bitter cold pierced the very heart of the ward. The furnace running full-time failed to repel the icy fingers. Petey knew the winter had arrived for good when he heard attendants and nurses wish each other Merry Christmas. He dreaded Christmas. Because nobody wanted to work then, Petey knew he would have to lie for hours in his waste before attendants had time to change the sheet under him.

By January, Petey's host of friends became an

even dozen. Sally's babies grew, and Petey became a very messy eater.

In mid-January, a new patient arrived on the ward. The attendants brought a nine-year-old boy over from the hospital in a wheelchair. They had discovered Calvin Anders, bruised and half-naked, abandoned on the front steps of the administration building during a snowstorm. He had been shivering and whimpering beside one of the large, marble pillars. Mildly retarded, with severe club feet, Calvin cowered from everyone.

Maybe because of their age or because of their wheelchairs, Petey and Calvin fascinated each other. At the ages of nine and twelve, they were the only children in an otherwise adult ward. Calvin sat for hours staring over at Petey and his wheelchair. His third day on the ward, Calvin scraped together his courage and headed his wheelchair toward Petey's corner of the room. Once in motion, Calvin was not a good driver. Twice he bumped into patients blocking his path. When they swore at him, Calvin grimaced and ducked his head as if avoiding stones. Petey watched Calvin intently as he approached.

"Ya been here long?" Calvin asked in a scared whisper.

Petey stared for a while and then nodded his head up and down, testing the old skill.

Calvin struggled to position his wheelchair in front of Petey, then looked up and down at him. He stared hard at the odd shapes under Petey's cover sheet. "What's wrong with you?" he whispered, scratching his black tousled hair.

Petey stared helplessly.

"Can't ya talk?"

Petey shook his head.

"You had an accident, didn't ya?"

Petey thought a moment—it *was* an accident of nature that made him this way. Hesitantly he jerked his chin in a nod. He smiled with excitement. For the first time in years he had communicated.

"Let's be friends," Calvin blurted, bouncing his chubby body up and down.

Again Petey jerked his head in a nod, smiling.

Throwing away the last of his caution, Calvin blurted, "I can get my bed moved over near yours. Is that okay?"

Petey grinned, nodding.

Calvin quickly learned Petey's name. Never taking no for an answer, he badgered every attendant or nurse who worked the ward. Finally he found one willing to arrange for him to sleep near Petey. The first night sounded like two children at a slumber party. Calvin kept whispering in the dark, while Petey smiled and grunted acknowledgment.

Twice Blackie and Patches tried to approach the wheelchair, but the talking scared them away. Petey couldn't wait to show Calvin his small friends. Late that night, before he fell asleep, he remembered seeing Sally, Cloud, and Esteban crawl up the wheelchair to eat. Once during the night he awoke to find Esteban curled next to his cheek. The little whiskers tickled him, and Petey smiled. Life was wonderful.

The next few weeks brimmed with discovery. Calvin, true to his nature, pestered the attendants until they pulled Petey next to the windows. Petey grinned and flailed his arms to show his approval.

Time spent with Calvin triggered dreams for Petey. He dreamed of playing with two children— one a girl, the other a boy. The dreams were so real. The vocabulary between Petey and Calvin also grew each day. Instead of simple nods, Petey's gestures became more subtle: a frown or smirk, the twitch of an eye, a wrinkled forehead. Every gesture became a thread woven into a larger tapestry. To help matters, Calvin slowly learned to ask questions that could be answered with a yes or no.

Petey tried to tell Calvin about his friends, the mice. Nothing made sense though. After several days of gesturing, Petey finally gave up.

One morning, a week later, Calvin rolled over to Petey after breakfast. "Hey, Petey," he said with his high-pitched, squeaky voice. "You shoulda seen all the mice on your wheelchair last night. I woke up and could see 'em in the light from the heater. There was a whole bunch."

Petey broke into a huge smile and nodded his head. "Aeee, aeee," he squealed. Looking up at the furnace and down at the floor he flopped his arms in glee.

"That's what you were telling me last week, wasn't it?" Calvin asked.

Petey smiled and squealed again, "Aeee, aeee."

"Maybe we can catch one," Calvin added.

Calvin's words caught Petey by surprise. He scowled, shaking his head no. "Oooo, oooo," he growled.

"We'll see," Calvin said mischievously.

That night, Calvin and Petey waited for the mice to come. Petey had been quite successful during supper at being messy. Shortly after the lights went out, the parade of mice began. First came Sally's five youngsters, followed by Sally herself. Next came the new gray mouse that Petey had named Sun. William and Cloud showed up about the same time over opposite sides of the chair. Then came Esteban, Blackie, and last of all Patches.

After a half hour of eating, Esteban crossed over to the bed and curled up next to Petey. Calvin could be seen blinking hard at the spectacle. Petey was prepared to flail his arms and grunt loudly if Calvin tried to catch or hurt any of his friends.

The next morning Calvin jabbered ecstatically. "You're actually friends with them, aren't ya?"

"Aeee, aeee," Petey cried.

"What's all the racket, boys?" the attendant,

Skully, asked as he approached. Both boys looked up with guilty stares, their secret intact. First the attendant helped Calvin get dressed and into his wheelchair. After sending him over for breakfast in the dayroom, he turned to Petey. "Okay, you're next." Reaching down to start cleaning, his eyes fell on Petey's cover sheet. He shouted over his shoulder, "Hey, Ed, come here a second."

The other attendant walked over. "What is it?"

"Look at this." Skully pulled off the sheet and roughly shook away the mouse droppings. "We need some rat poison."

Chapter 6

As Petey was wheeled over to the dayroom for breakfast, his mind raced. He knew what poison meant from idle talk overheard in Infants' Ward, but he had no idea what poison looked like. The attendant's hard shakes of the sheet, however, made it clear the mice would not be tolerated.

Waiting for food, Petey sat with his head angled sharply over to the left as if frozen at the end of a stretch. Somehow he had to keep food off his sheet. Opening his mouth extra wide, he concentrated on each bite. Desperately he curled his lips around the food. His enormous effort was not entirely successful. Choking and gagging on the trapped food, he finally wrenched his head sideways and spewed a mouthful all over the floor. Some hit the attendant.

"Knock that off!" the man bellowed. "You act like you've never eaten before."

Petey curled his lips inward and examined the sheet. Although still hungry, he decided not to push his luck. He closed his mouth to the next bite and shook his head back and forth.

"Okay, suits me," the attendant declared, shoving back from the table.

All morning Petey tried to communicate his problem to Calvin, but the concept was too complicated. What gestures explained rat poison or mouse droppings? Finally he gave up in hopeless despair and ignored Calvin's probing questions. Calvin rolled away to a different window.

By supper, Petey was so hungry he had to eat something. Twice, his coughing spells sprayed food in every direction. After the meal he inspected his sheet. Several large food bits lay scattered near his waist. He flung his arms and twisted his body. The food bits moved, but fell against his legs where he could force no motion. All evening he stared down at the morsels, each one representing death to his tiny friends.

When at last the attendant lifted him onto his bed for the night, Petey was exhausted. The day's efforts only made the upcoming vigil more torturous. As the light switched off, Petey listened in the dark for any sound of his friends. Once a faint shuffle sounded on the hard floor and Petey convulsed his body. The sound disappeared. When the furnace first kicked on, he saw William nosing his whiskers over the edge of the chair. Petey flailed his arms wildly and watched his friend scamper away.

Three more times during the night he grunted and struggled against sounds from the darkness. Finally, Petey could no longer keep his eyes open and submitted to his weariness. He slept until the furnace roared to life and jarred him awake. Skimming his eyes back and forth across the sheet, Petey sighed with relief—he spotted no movement. Then he looked down in horror. A little furry pile had curled up next to his leg. Esteban!

Petey watched the small mouse for several long

minutes. Esteban cuddled closer and tucked his tiny nose snugly between his feet. Twice Petey tried to strike out at his friend, but his body froze and refused the act. Esteban trusted him and would not understand this act of betrayal. Petey's feelings tore at his conscience. Any further stillness condemned Esteban to death. Finally with a sudden jerk, Petey closed his eyes and brought his arms crashing against his leg near where the little mouse slept.

Esteban scrambled frantically out of his cozy nest as Petey's arms pummeled him, sending him tumbling to the floor. Petey let out a pinched cry and continued flailing his bent arms in a frenzy. He kept his eyes closed.

One bed away, Calvin had awakened to find Petey lashing out at the mouse that so often cuddled near his side. Even after the little mouse hit the floor and scurried away, Calvin watched Petey whip his arms up and down, eyes closed tightly in a grimace.

The next morning, wake-up call came like a sentry, relieving Petey of duty. Light snow flecked against the dirty window panes. Petey was glad not having to get up. Before he closed his eyes to sleep again, he looked over at the large melting droplets creeping their way down the glass. They were huge teardrops that refused to stop.

The bright ceiling lights and the attendant's grating voice kept clawing Petey rudely from his sleep. His body felt heavy with fatigue and retreated back into a stuporous slumber. The rough shake of a hand jarred Petey. "Hey, guy, join the living!"

Petey stared morosely as the attendant stripped his blanket off and rolled him over for cleaning.

All day Petey heard no mention made of the mice or poison, but he knew all the attendants needed was a reminder. Except at feeding time, Petey slept soundly in his chair. Calvin tried unsuccessfully to ask Petey about his actions the night before. Petey closed his eyes, too exhausted to answer. The bedlam rising from the ward blanketed his sleep, and not until supper did Petey open his eyes and gaze dully about the room.

Patients moved past, conducting themselves with their usual confusing movements and unknown intentions. Calvin sat across the ward staring into space. Petey watched him, wishing somehow he could explain the problem. Finally Calvin broke from his fixed gaze and turned to look. Petey smiled to show friendship.

Hesitantly Calvin wheeled himself across the ward. "Hey, Petey, are ya awake?" he asked, as he came near.

"Aeee, aeee."

"Why are ya mad at me?"

"Oooo, oooo."

"You mean you ain't mad at me?"

"Oooo."

"Then how come you wouldn't talk to me this morning? And why did ya chase the mouse off your bed last night? And why did ya sleep all day?"

Petey looked back at Calvin with a helpless stare. His eyes pleaded for questions he could answer.

"I know, you can't tell me," Calvin reminded himself. "Not unless I can guess, huh?"

Petey nodded.

For several minutes they regarded each other

before Calvin spoke. "Okay, then, lemme try."
He wrinkled his forehead and puzzled. His little
club feet strained inward as if to aid the effort.
"Did ya hit the mouse 'cause he did something
to you?"

"Oooo."

"Were you mad at him?"

"Oooo, oooo."

"Then why did ya swing at the mouse?"

Petey gave Calvin a look of reproach.

"Okay, okay, were ya helping the mouse?"

Petey broke into a smile. "Aeee, aeee."

"Petey, you're screwy. You don't help a mouse
by hitting it."

Petey nodded his head insistently.

"Petey, I don't understand." Again Calvin sat
puzzling for some time before he spoke again.
"Were ya trying to chase it away?"

Petey nodded.

"You were trying to help the mouse by chasing
it away?"

"Aeee, aeee."

"That don't make sense."

Petey sat helpless.

"Was something gonna hurt the mouse?" Calvin ventured.

Petey nodded his head eagerly. "Aeee, aeee."

"What was gonna hurt 'im?"

Petey stared.

"Was it someone?"

"Aeee."

"Who?"

Petey frowned and shifted his eyes over toward the nurses' station.

"They were gonna hurt the mice—the attendants?"

"Aeee."

"How could they hurt the mice?"

Petey could only stare at Calvin.

"Were they gonna put out mousetraps?"

Petey thought for a moment. Calvin almost had the answer in hand. If he said no, Calvin might give up, and they would never again return within reach of the proper answer. But Petey trusted Calvin's persistence and felt certain he would not give up. Petey bet everything on his reply. "Oooo, oooo."

"You mean they were gonna hurt the mice, but

they weren't gonna set mousetraps?"

"Aeee."

"Petey, you're really screwy. They can't hurt mice if they don't set mousetraps."

Now Petey worried. Maybe Calvin didn't know about poison. He looked at Calvin with a pleading look, begging him to keep trying.

"How else can they hurt the mice, Petey?"

Petey waited silently.

Calvin bit at his lip and scratched both sides of his head. Finally he threw his arms up. "I don't know, maybe with poison."

Petey jerked his arms wildly. His face lit up with a smile and he squealed his answer. "Aeee! Aeee! Aeee!"

"They're gonna use poison? They said that?"

"Aeee." Petey jerked his chin up and down. His excitement went beyond the poison. Today he had successfully communicated a thought. He had broken through the invincible barrier guarding his mind.

Chapter 7

After supper, Calvin's interrogation of Petey continued. He finally determined that food on Petey's sheet had lured the mice. "I'll clean your sheet before we go to bed," Calvin said, "and stay awake to help chase away the mice."

"Guuu, guuu," Petey grunted.

" 'Cause I can wake you up easier, let me watch first."

Petey nodded.

That night, Petey fell asleep even before the lights were off. It seemed only minutes before Calvin's voice stole into his dreams. "Hey, Petey, wake up."

Petey blinked, staring into the darkness.

"Wake up, Petey, it's your turn. I can't stay awake no more. I chased away three mice. Are you awake, Petey?"

"Aeee, aeee," Petey squeaked as quietly as he could.

For a week the watch continued. Soon the mice quit coming. Except for Calvin brushing crumbs from Petey's sheet, the two no longer kept their nightly vigil. Petey missed his little friends and worried about Esteban and Sally, his two favorites. They had been like a family. Now their loss brought painful tears. Petey craved a family. It was as if his mind knew of love and devotion, but the feelings must have been only his imagination. Nothing Petey remembered was ever so special.

Calvin had satisfied part of this void. Though retarded, his shortcomings were offset by sheer determination. Calvin doggedly deciphered Petey's grunts and gestures until he captured basic notions. With effort he wove the notions like threads into an idea, eventually forming a concept. Once captured, Petey and Calvin paraded the shared understanding back and forth between them like proud captors of a snared rabbit.

Calvin's tenacity made him a dreaded presence on the ward. His endless questions and opinions tested each patient's endurance. In his spare time, Calvin began disassembling everything he touched. He never quite remembered how to reassemble his destruction. The last straw fell the day he reduced his wheelchair to scattered tires, pads, tubes, and a headrest.

"Calvin!" the attendant scolded. "Knock it off! You take one more thing apart, I'll take your wheelchair away and you can stay in bed—you hear me?"

Reluctantly Calvin agreed. After that he began grabbing the handles on Petey's wheelchair and shoving him a few feet. Wheeling himself forward, he repeated this motion. Soon Calvin could position both chairs near the windows without depending on the attendant. He spent full afternoons pushing Petey around the ward.

One day Calvin spun Petey in circles. Petey flailed his arms and grunted to stop, but Calvin spun him faster and faster. When he finally let the dizzy Petey roll to a stop, Petey threw up all over himself.

"Oh, boy!" Calvin exclaimed. "If you did that when I was spinning you, it would have splattered everyone!"

Petey mustered his most severe scowl.

Late one afternoon Calvin wheeled up to Petey. "Hey, Petey, I been thinking. You gotta learn more words. If you can say yes, no, and good, you can say other stuff, too."

Petey shook his head, but as he sat alone staring out the windows he began mouthing words he'd heard. It took so much effort to close his lips he could not make a sound at the same time—his throat felt like something gripped it in a clamp. The biggest problem was his tongue. Jutting sideways in his mouth, the tongue gnarled about, defying any command. When forming words, it fell short of contacting the top of his mouth, leaving air to rush past. It helped to press his bottom lip against his upper gum. Petey realized the best way to make any good sound was the way he said "Aeee," "Oooo," and "Guuu." He had to use his throat.

The first success came with the words "pretty good." Squirreling his cheeks back and almost humming, he grunted out a very rough, "Pfer guuu." He could utter this without using his tongue. Over and over he practiced.

The next morning Calvin wheeled over. "Hi, Petey, how you doing?"

"Pfer guuu!" Petey grunted.

Calvin stared.

"Pfer guuu."

Calvin tipped his head sideways. "You telling me something?"

Petey nodded.

Calvin skewed his face thoughtfully and scratched his head. "Let me think. . . . I asked how you was doing, and you said, 'Pfer guuu.' You mean pretty good?"

"Aeee, aeee."

Calvin broke out laughing.

Petey smiled and puckered his cheeks again in a guttural, but jubilant, "Pfer guuu! Pfer guuu!"

The next day, Petey learned the word *good-bye*.

Unable to say good night, this was the nearest thing he could think of. Again it exacted great effort, but he grunted out a coarse, "Guuu baa." Before long the whole ward listened each night to the good-night salutation conducted in the two corner beds.

"Good night, Petey."

"Guuu baa."

The joy of learning to communicate with Calvin helped temper Petey's loss of the mice. But Petey worried about Calvin. The boy either boiled over with motion and laughter or sat secluded in total silence. Some days he spent whole mornings at the dayroom table, slumped over, head tucked in his arms.

Each day, Petey sat silently by the window. Often he watched the round glass thing on the wall. During the last year the object had captivated his attention, holding him spellbound for long hours at a time. The device had two little levers or rods. One of the levers was longer than the other. The longest one went around and around, maybe a dozen or more times each day.

The shorter one barely moved. If lucky, it went around once. Petey learned to predict mealtimes by watching the levers.

Watching the movement of the levers became more satisfying than looking out the windows. The windows left him longing to reach out his hand and touch the wind, or feel the sun against his face. The old memories of his trip over from Infants' Ward had dulled in his mind, and with each rotation of the lever, the memories came more from imagination. Maybe he had never really felt the sun and wind.

One day, blustery weather rolled in over the grounds. Wind howled down from a threatening sky. As Calvin and Petey sat together at the far end of the ward, Calvin began clowning around. "Look how I can spin," he said, pushing opposite directions on his tires. The chair rammed the wall and tipped over. Calvin pitched forward and fell from the chair. With a dull thud, his head hit the wooden floor. He groaned and struggled to get up, then collapsed and lay still.

Petey grunted and tried to wave his arms but

nobody noticed. He sat frozen in numbed silence. His best friend needed help, and all he could do was sit helplessly in his wheelchair and grunt like an idiot.

Chapter 8

Calvin lay deathly still. Try as he might, Petey could think of no way to help his friend. He cursed his useless body. All it could do was choke on food when he tried to eat, and hours later make a mess that somebody else had to clean. Anger filled Petey. He was alive and he could think—that was worth something! Somehow he must help Calvin. And soon!

Suddenly, Petey drew in a deep breath, shooting a sharp pang into his chest. Then doing something he had never dared before, he forced air into his stiff, pinched throat. A siren squeal pierced the air. Grimacing, Petey thrashed his arms, hitting the wall and window moldings. Jolts of pain bit at his wrists, and black darkness drowned his vision. Still he flailed his arms.

Two powerful hands grasped Petey's arms. Petey opened his eyes to look up at the attendant.

"Hey! Hey! Hey! Hold on, fellow. I'm here. I'll get help for Calvin!" The attendant shouted across the ward to the other attendant, "Go get help!"

Petey watched as the huge man crouched over Calvin's motionless body and felt for a pulse. Calvin groaned and tried to sit up. Grimacing, he reached for his head. "I hit a truck," he grunted.

In minutes a nurse ran in. Except for a fist-sized knot on his head, Calvin was okay. The big attendant eyed Petey as if sorting out a puzzle in his mind. "That was good what you did," he said, examining Petey's scraped and bruised hands. "Let's get something for the cuts." When the attendant returned with bandages, he squeezed Petey's shoulder. "You sure ain't no idiot."

Petey smiled, then closed his eyes and again let darkness bathe his mind and body.

Later, Calvin wheeled over to where Petey lay

spent and hurting. "Uh, Petey, I . . . I heard what you did for me. Thanks." Calvin looked down. "Petey, you're my best friend."

Again Petey smiled and forced a nod. "I didn't know you could scream," Calvin blurted.

The big attendant, Joe, who had come to Calvin's rescue, had started working on the ward only a few days earlier. Joe had muddy-brown hair, a squared jaw, and walked a bit slowly—as if each step pained him. Within a few days, Calvin wrangled out of him his name and life history.

Joe had worked for years on the Milwaukee and Northern Pacific railroads as a gandy dancer, pounding railroad spikes to the gandy's cadence. A disease in Joe's muscles finally made it too painful to swing his hammer any longer. But still he hummed the songs of the railroad.

As the summer of 1937 faded into autumn, Joe's strength ebbed. By first snow, simple tasks demanded monumental effort. Petey noticed Joe's decline but had no idea what was wrong.

"What you got planned today?" Joe asked one morning as he grunted to roll Petey facedown for cleaning. Pressure on Petey's chest kept him from answering. Joe filled in the silence. "Gonna put soup on my chair again?"

Petey grinned. Last month, Joe had brought a bowl of soup into the dayroom for a feeding. Seeing the table cluttered with trays and plates, he set the bowl on the bench while he returned to the food cart for a spoon. On returning, he accidentally sat squarely in the bowl of steaming chicken-noodle broth. Petey had howled laughing as Joe leaped up in surprise, britches hot and dripping.

"You sure have grown, buddy," Joe said, allowing Petey to flop again onto his back. "You're a teenager now."

"Aeee," Petey said.

Joe grimaced as he hefted Petey into the wheel-chair. "I'll bet you weigh a hundred and twenty," he said, breathing heavily.

Petey eyed his big friend fondly. After rescuing Calvin, Joe had become like a father. Nobody on the ward messed with Petey or Calvin without answering to Joe.

"I don't know how much longer I can keep working," Joe said sadly.

"Whaaaee?" Petey pleaded.

Joe shook his head, not answering. With a loving tweak on the chin, he pushed Petey into the dayroom for breakfast. As usual, Calvin waited at one corner of the table, his wheelchair crowded out by patients already devouring their meals. Seeing Joe and Petey enter the room, Calvin extended his index finger like a pistol and clicked his throat in mock gunfire. "Ke, ke, ke."

Petey smiled and flailed his arms, returning the gunfire. "Kkkk, kkkk."

Laughing, Calvin turned his pretend gunfire on Joe. Petey joined in, helping spray their big friend with imaginary bullets. Joe clutched his chest with one hand and steadied his mortally wounded body with the other.

Petey watched Joe reeling in mock pain. This game had started a few months earlier when the attendants started bringing a big machine up to the ward that shined a bright light against the wall. When the other lights were turned out, people could be seen moving and talking on the wall, like magic. The machine could even make horses and buildings appear. Joe called them movies.

Every week Petey and Calvin looked forward to Friday night. Joe sat between them and gave names to the magical people, names like Hoot Gibson, Tom Mix, and Gary Cooper. The boys remembered their favorite movies, *The Wild West, The Virginian, Death Valley, The Big Trail,* and *Billy the Kid.*

Petey assumed that somehow this machine showed things as they actually happened elsewhere. But one night he watched *The Texan* for the second time. Puzzled looks and gestures finally coaxed an explanation out of Joe. Somehow the big reels of tape held the people and could show them over and over.

Petey and Calvin loved the movies with cowboys. Their favorite cowboys never got killed in gunfights. After each show, the boys faked pistol battles. Their wheelchairs became magnificent galloping stallions. The dirty, crowded ward, filled with beds, became a sun-streaked landscape, criss-crossed by mountains and canyons. Docile patients staring out windows became unsuspecting members of many a roundup posse. Old Zeke, a bedridden miner halfway down the ward from Petey and Calvin, had helped them rob seventeen banks, escape from as many jails, and kill a dozen bandits—all without leaving his bed or suspecting his involvement. Calvin, able to move his wheelchair, did all the sneaking, often running into other patients as he escaped the pursuing posse.

Still clutching at his chest, Joe interrupted the morning's shoot-out. "Okay, you two, nobody dies until after breakfast," he ordered. "I hate feeding dead people." Joe parked Petey next to Calvin, then brought oatmeal from the cart and set it on the table.

Petey liked oatmeal. It was one of the few times he ate his food the same as everyone else. Usually his food had to be ground through a meat grinder. Each week the menu remained the same. Because of this, Petey knew that for lunch today they would get meat loaf and corn—for him this would be ground into a burnt colored pudding with yellow specks, not too unlike his oatmeal.

Petey yawned, feeling unusually spent from his short gun battle. He ignored the weariness, but after only a few bites, he felt nauseated and warm.

He signaled Joe he was full. By mid-morning, Petey had uncontrollable chills and big drops of sweat beading his forehead. After Calvin killed Petey three times without a single shot in defense, he wheeled near. "Hey, Petey, I didn't really shoot you! Are ya okay? You don't look so good."

"Oooo, oooo." Petey shook his head, grimacing.

"I'll get Joe, he'll help you." Calvin angled across the ward, cranking furiously at the wheels and hollering, "Hey, Joe! Hey, Joe! Hey, Joe!" Patients scattered, each harboring memories of bruised shins and pinched toes on Calvin's account. Soon, Calvin returned with Joe.

"What's wrong, Petey? Not feeling good?" Joe asked, concern in his face.

"Owwwwwee," Petey whimpered.

"Let's get a blanket over you and call the doctor." Joe sent the other attendant to summon the doctor as Calvin wheeled himself frantically across the ward. "I'll get him my blanket," Calvin shouted. Once more patients scattered, flinging obscenities and hazarding remarks from the protection of their beds. Joe smiled. A blanket lay not ten feet from where he stood, but he couldn't deny Calvin his gesture of friendship.

After a long wait, a thin, bony doctor arrived, toting his big black bag. He wore a loose, almost sloppy, gray suit. The doctor shook his head at the sight of Petey. "Poor fellow. Got some bug, huh? Well, let's see what it is." The entire ward turned their attention to the doctor's visit.

The doctor pulled back the blanket and opened Petey's shirt to expose his chest. Twice he placed a thermometer in Petey's mouth, but Petey's coiled tongue rejected its presence. Finally he slipped his hand underneath the sheet and placed the thermometer where it could not be rejected, much to Petey's dismay. Next he touched his stethoscope to Petey's chest and listened. A hush fell over the ward as fifty other patients helped listen.

After retrieving the thermometer and completing his examination, the doctor glanced over Petey's medical records. He set his bag on the edge of the bed. "We have one sick boy here," he said, producing several bottles and doling out measured portions of foul-tasting liquid, along with several pills.

Before leaving he turned to Joe, who sat holding

Petey's hand. "He's got a good case of flu and pneumonia. I've given him some tonic and tinctures. Considering he's an idiot, I wouldn't get my hopes too high. These kind seldom live long anyway."

"This child is no idiot," Joe said firmly.

The doctor raised a stern finger. "Don't let your fondness of a patient jade your perception. This child *is* an idiot. You cannot change that fact."

After making note of the doctor's instructions, Joe watched him leave, then murmured, "You're no idiot, Petey. You'll still be around years from now when that doctor is belly up to a gravestone."

Chapter 9

For several weeks Petey's weakened body fought the infection. Joe made sure every attendant knew what special care was needed. He assigned Calvin the job of dispensing water and keeping Petey's face wiped with a damp cloth. In time, Petey dreaded seeing Calvin approach with more water. So diligent was Calvin at dispensing fluids that nearly every hour an attendant had to change Petey's wet pads. Calvin stroked Petey's forehead and face until the skin became raw and Joe had to curb his zeal.

Petey slipped in and out of consciousness,

sweating, then shivering. Calvin's constant babble annoyed him. He wished his chubby friend would just go away and let him drift into a deep, endless sleep.

During Petey's long illness, Joe often stopped after his shift to sit and talk. Petey clung doggedly to consciousness, trying to listen. One night as the big man stood wearily to leave, Petey deliberately grunted the words, "Guuu baa, Cho."

Joe looked down surprised. "You can say my name?"

Petey nodded, smiling weakly.

Joe looked down in puzzled silence. "Good night, Petey. It's been real good talking," he said.

Petey nodded.

Joe's walk was unsteady, and his shoulders sagged as he left the ward.

Petey remained deathly ill, overwhelmed with hacking coughs, chills, and delirium. When the first sign of recovery came, it happened under the cover of night. Petey stopped his restless shivering and fell into a deep, heavy sleep. When morning tried to wake him, sleep reclaimed his body several times. He finally awoke feeling hunger, his first hunger in over a month.

Soon Petey and Calvin again played cowboys by the hour, clicking and clicking at each other in mock battle. In the spirit of sportsmanship, Calvin tried not to sound out any louder than Petey. Once in a while, however, he screamed loudly in the frenzy of battle, "Bang! Bang! Bang!" When every eye in the ward turned toward him, he'd lower his head and return meekly to a subdued "Ke, ke, ke."

With the coming of winter, cold winds clawed at the ward once more. The furnace cycled frantically against the relentless chill. One snowy evening, Joe visited the ward. While patients prepared for bed, he stopped beside Petey and Calvin, a bag in his arms. "Hey, guys, you know what day it is?"

Petey and Calvin looked up curiously. "Tuesday?" Calvin ventured.

"No, no, no. I mean what's special about this day?"

"Today we had jelly sandwiches."

Joe shook his head.

"Waa? Waa?" Petey grunted.

"It's Christmas Eve." Seeing the boys' blank stares, Joe explained. "Listen, you guys, Christmas is a time of peace, happiness, and celebration. This is when we remember that all people are brothers and sisters."

"We don't have no family," Calvin said glumly.

"You have me. That's why I came here tonight, to bring you gifts." Joe pulled out two colorfully wrapped packages from his bag. He held them back from Calvin's impatient reach. "You can't open them until morning, when I come on shift; that way you have all night to dream about them. Dreamin' is half the fun."

Petey and Calvin looked at each other, giddy with excitement.

"You know what these are?" Joe asked, pulling two big socks from the pocket of his heavy jacket.

"Yeah," Calvin blurted. "Big, dirty socks!"

Joe laughed. "These are more than big, dirty socks. We're gonna hang them up in the nurses' station. If you've both been good this year maybe

Santa Claus will put candy in them. I'll help you check them in the morning."

"Santa Claus is a big fat guy dressed in red," Calvin announced.

"And he gives presents to good people," Joe added.

When Joe first mentioned Christmas, Petey had not been excited. Now, with the prospect of socks and presents, he grinned widely. He could not envision the toys most children conjured up—but this did not dampen the intrigue. Late into the night he grunted excitedly. Calvin announced repeatedly, "I think I'm going to get a horse."

After threats from other weary patients, Petey and Calvin drifted into fitful but enchanted sleep. They dreamed about brightly colored boxes, dirty socks, and a big fat guy dressed in red.

Long before wake-up call, Calvin called loudly, "Hey, Petey, it's Christmas! Today we get our presents!"

Petey opened his eyes, instantly awake and fully aware of the suspense this day held.

"You two shut up!" growled one of the patients. "Or you won't live to open presents!"

Quietly the boys waited. Finally Joe arrived for his 6 A.M. shift. He walked slowly, like an old man.

Calvin hollered to him as he entered the ward. "Hey, Joe, it's Christmas!"

Joe gasped, faking surprise. "It is? Well, let's get up and about then. No presents till after breakfast."

Devouring the fastest meal ever consumed on the ward, Petey and Calvin waited anxiously as Joe finished his duties. After what seemed like an eternity, Joe finally accompanied the boys to the nurses' station. First he placed a gift on Petey's chest. Petey gave him a helpless, expectant look.

"I'm not opening that for you," Joe said.

"Aeee, aeee," Petey squeaked his concern.

"I'll help, but you gotta help, too." Joe lifted Petey's limp hand and held one of his stiff fingers like a letter opener. Petey stared as he felt his finger rip open the paper. Calvin squirmed impatiently, like a puppy with bacon dangling in front of his nose. With Petey's gift almost open, Joe handed Calvin his. Calvin shredded the wrapped box instantly.

Both boys had received a leather holster and

belt. Each holster held a brand new silver toy pistol.

"Oh, boy, Petey, look at these!" Calvin shrieked.

Petey grinned and flapped his arms. "Ohh booee!"

Joe smiled, watching the two boys. As Calvin put his belt on, Joe reached over and mounted Petey's holster on the side of his wheelchair. Carefully he attached the pistol to Petey's wrist with rubber bands.

Immediately the boys started a fusillade of "Kkkk, kkkk, kkkk," and "Ke, ke, ke." Luckily, Petey didn't have to aim well, or his bullets would have hit the ceiling.

Joe smiled as he watched his young friends play. Had they not been crippled and confined to this asylum, they were old enough now to drive cars, date, play sports, and get jobs. An intense joy filled Joe as he watched Petey sit stationary in the middle of the room with Calvin lunging his wheelchair around in circles. Both teenagers clicked their throats furiously, arms swinging.

Calvin halted his play. "Joe. How about the socks?"

Joe shrugged. "I don't know, Calvin, they might be empty. Santa only leaves things for people who are good."

"We've been good, at least I have," Calvin vowed. "I don't know about Petey."

Joe looked over at Petey. "Well, have you been good?"

A smile flooded Petey's face, and his arms jerked wildly. "Pfer guuu! Pfer guuu!"

Joe retrieved the two socks stuffed with candy. In Petey's sock, Joe had added a small, framed piece of paper. "Waa?" Petey asked, looking at the framed paper.

"That, Petey, is a special gift for you."

"Waa? Waa?"

"Here, I'll read it to you." Joe read slowly, "'They who wait for the Lord shall renew their strength, they shall mount up with wings like eagles, they shall run and not be weary, they shall walk and not faint.'"

"What's an eagle?" Calvin blurted.

"Well, it's like the pigeons we have around here, only much bigger," Joe explained.

"Joe, I like pigeons better," Calvin commented.

"Don't you, Petey? Cripes, are they fast."

"Aeee, aeee."

Joe looked at the two boys, then shook his head, chuckling. "Okay, we'll fix that." He grabbed a pen from the nurses' station and made a correction on the framed paper. "Okay, how does this sound? 'They shall mount up with wings like pigeons.'"

"Yeah, that's better," Calvin exclaimed.

"What do you think, Petey?" Joe enquired.

"Aeee. Pfer guuu, pfer guuu."

Later that day, during a lull in one of their pitched battles, Petey motioned for Calvin to come near.

"What you want, Petey?" Calvin asked.

Petey motioned toward the shredded Christmas paper and the socks filled with candy. Next he motioned toward Joe working at the far end of the ward. "Kkk mah, kkk mah," Petey repeated insistently.

After puzzling a minute, Calvin realized that Petey wanted to give Joe a Christmas present. With an air of mischief, both boys donated candy from their socks and Calvin wrapped it awkwardly in the biggest piece of colored paper they could salvage. Then, hiding it behind his back, Calvin yelled, "Hey, Joe! Come here!"

When Joe arrived, Calvin thrust the hidden gift forward. "It's from me and Petey."

"What in the world is this?" Joe feigned surprise as he opened the little bundle and discovered the candy.

"Merry Christmas," Calvin blurted.

Reaching down, Joe hugged each boy. "Merry Christmas, you two. A bountiful Merry Christmas."

Chapter 10

Joe devoted his last months to Petey and Calvin. It pained them to watch such a large, commanding figure—and faithful friend—deteriorate until nurses half his size were summoned to lift his patients. His leaving became inevitable, aided by his stubborn will to depart while he could still walk, his head held high.

In late spring, Joe worked his final shift on the ward. He said good-bye to Petey and Calvin with a simple pat on the shoulder and a loving tweak on the chin. "Take good care of yourselves" were his last words.

Then he was gone.

Joe's departure devastated Petey and Calvin. No amount of tears could bring him back. Several letters from hospitals in Portland and Seattle arrived for the boys. A nurse read the letters to them. In each letter Joe talked about oceans and ships and big cities, but never about his ailment. When six months passed without a letter, each boy quietly accepted the implication.

Without Joe, seasons cycled without remorse. After each bleak winter, springtime winds tumbled in over the Rockies, warming the harsh landscape and melting snow cover. Just as the cold had pried past the large single-pane windows each winter, so did spring warmth creep gently into the ward. Days grew longer, but daybreak and sunset still traded light with their passionless rhythm. Time plodded forward.

Petey endured time gazing halfheartedly out through dirty windows. Shafts of light poked into the room, falling onto a worn and discolored floor. The yellow varnish had chips and scrapes, which over the years had allowed the wood to absorb anything it touched. Now the floor doled out these odors of urine, spilled food, lye, sweat, and vomit. The smell left many newcomers queasy, but the patients hardly noticed. They had long ago become a part of the waste.

The passing of time also tormented Petey's body, continuing the cruel havoc that nature had introduced at birth. Petey's small legs grew, tugging in tighter against his chest. His right leg slowly crossed the left, leaving both knees angled upward. Petey's head pitched sideways, and his arms and wrists drew in like chicken wings. When he grew excited, his shriveled limbs thrashed about like a big featherless bird trying to take flight.

Calvin became a daily fixture at the far corner of the dayroom, his head cradled in his arms, face down. After Joe had left, two years earlier, Calvin withdrew into a troubled world of silence. His weight ballooned until he resembled a Buddha statue with distorted legs facing inward. His silver pistol, handle worn smooth from use, gathered dust on his green metal nightstand. Occasionally a reluctant game of cowboy brought half smiles, but it also triggered memories of Joe leaving. The memories plunged Calvin deeper into his self-imposed exile.

Other changes followed Joe's leaving. Now Petey found himself cared for by women. Because of war against the Germans and Japanese, most able-bodied male attendants had left, replaced by older men, women, or nursing students taking psychiatric training at Warm Springs.

One of the women who worked on Ward 18, Cassie Graber, was an attractive twenty-four-year-old nurse. Her husband, drafted after the attack on Pearl Harbor, left for Europe not knowing she was pregnant with their first child. Life for Cassie was a tedium of long shifts, caring for her little girl, Lisa, and writing letters to her husband, Alex. Her only respite from the monotony was the unbelievably deformed, but delightful, twenty-two-year-old patient named Petey Corbin. Officially he was diagnosed an idiot. Unofficially, she discovered him to be a wonderful human being. They quickly became close friends.

One day as Petey stared silently out the window, Cassie walked up behind him quietly and laid her hand softly on his shoulder. "A penny for your thoughts."

Petey jerked at the surprise touch, flailing his arms. The restraint that usually stops such a reflex in most people was missing from Petey's development. His surprise gave way to a huge smile of recognition. "Aaooo," he countered, grinning up at the blonde nurse.

"You look kinda bored."

"Oooo." Actually he was bored numb, but one touch from Cassie made Petey anything but bored. "Hhoo yoo phaephy?" he asked.

"My baby?"

"Aeee."

"Lisa is doing just fine, Petey. Maybe tomorrow I'll bring her in again and show you how she's grown."

"Pfer guuu, pfer guuu." Petey motioned with concerned eyes to where Calvin sat despondently. After Joe left, Petey's emptiness had been filled by Cassie. She came to the ward like a breath of sunshine, fussing over him and joking to cheer him up. For Calvin the emptiness remained.

"You worried about Calvin?" Cassie asked.

"Aeee."

"So am I, Petey. I'm not sure what to do for him. It seems that after people lose friends they often lose their reason to exist. What Calvin has to learn is that there is always tomorrow and new friends."

"Aeee."

"You understand that?"

"Aeee."

"I know you do, Petey. Well, I gotta get busy. I'll try to bring Lisa in tomorrow. It's my day off."

"Eeesa."

"That's right, Petey, Lisa." As she turned to leave she ruffled Petey's hair. "See ya, buddy."

"Guuu baa."

Petey strained to watch her leave. She walked like a big beautiful cat, her gently curved body firm and captivating. Strange and exciting feelings stole Petey's breath away when Cassie smiled or patted his forehead. Often he dreamed of walking down the long path from Infants' Ward holding hands with Cassie. Whenever he reached Men's Ward, he always woke up to his crippled body and a wheelchair beside the bed. Some night maybe his dream would take him off that path. He'd walk with Cassie out across the open field behind the ward and never return.

The rest of the morning Petey stared into space, engrossed in thought. Occasionally his uncontrolled jerks helped chase away flies that crawled into his ears or nose. Shortly after lunch he needed changing. Accustomed to sitting in this condition for hours, he tried not to think about it. Finally, late in the afternoon, Cassie bustled over. She wore a starched blouse tucked into a long white skirt. "Petey, I've been so busy. Do you need changing?"

Reluctantly, Petey nodded.

As Cassie wheeled him to his bed, Petey looked up at the gentle face above him. Several loose strands of Cassie's long hair dangled over her shoulders. Sometimes, when she bent over, the hair drifted across Petey's face. His body shivered as if touched by wind. He never grew tired of admiring Cassie.

The bump of his chair against the bed woke him rudely from his state of adoration. Aided by another nurse, Cassie swung Petey onto the bed for changing. Petey had never felt embarrassed lying helpless, exposed, and in need of cleaning—not until Cassie came along. All of a sudden he was filled with a shame he could not explain or escape from.

Again and again he told himself that the hands that cleaned him were not Cassie's touch; they were from the person whose job it was to care for him. Cassie's touch was the hand on his cheek, the warm smile that shortened his breath as she stroked his forehead. But try as he might, the thought haunted Petey: what did Cassie think of him as she cleaned his deformed, helpless body? He feared the answer.

Wearing only a shirt and socks, Petey was lifted awkwardly back into the chair. Quickly Cassie pulled the white sheet up over his bent legs and tucked in the ends. When Cassie was there, the sheet could never be pulled up fast enough or tucked in far enough. Safely covered, Petey looked up shyly. "Thaaa uuu."

"Oh, you're welcome." Cassie smiled as if meeting a handsome prince. "Hey, Petey, tomorrow when I bring Lisa over, would you like to go outside?"

Petey stared in disbelief. Outside! Was she teasing him? "Waaaee, waaaee?"

"Why?"

"Aeee."

"Well, tomorrow the Montana State College band is coming to perform. They're playing out by the pond. Because it's my day off I'll have the time to help bring you down. Would you like that?"

"Aeee! Aeee! Aeee!" Petey gasped.

"Okay, I'll see you tomorrow."

As she turned to leave, Petey looked over to where Calvin sat despondently beside the table. "Woooo! Woooo!"

Cassie turned back. "What did you say? Whoa?"

Petey nodded, smiling, then glanced toward Calvin.

"You want to know if Calvin can go along, don't you?"

"Aeee, aeee."

Cassie eyed Petey with admiration, then reached and squeezed his shoulder. "You're always thinking of others. Of course Calvin can go. It will be good for him."

"Aeee, aeee."

As Cassie left the ward, Petey watched her every move and followed her until the last stitch of her white dress disappeared out the door.

The rest of that day and late into the night, Petey dreamed of two things: of Cassie and of going outside. He had not been outside since coming from Infants' Ward many, many long years before. The very thought left him dizzy with excitement.

Chapter 11

Petey awoke before daybreak. Aching with anticipation, he watched the burnished windowpanes grow lighter, changing shades of gray. Imperceptibly at first, then vividly, the windows blushed crimson until they glowed.

Petey's memories of being outside were old and faded by time—no longer real. Now the slow arrival of morning taunted him. It would be hours before Cassie came. Second by second, Petey endured the long wait.

Finally, he heard Cassie's voice. "Hey, tiger. Are

you ready?" she called, crossing the ward.

Petey grinned and nodded, then motioned toward Calvin.

"We'll come back and get him."

"Guuu, guuu."

As attendants jostled Petey down the long flight of concrete stairs, Cassie walked alongside, carrying her baby. She wore a colorful blue-flowered dress with frilly short sleeves that made her appear to float as she walked. Her hair hung loose, cascading over her shoulders. Petey forgot to breathe.

Outside, a blinding sun greeted them. Eager patients herded past on either side. Squinting, Petey's eyes darted back and forth. Automobiles honked, racing past on a smooth black surface that hid the dirt. The air, fresh and fragrant, coursed over Petey, tickling his body. Elated, Petey flailed his arms.

Cassie found a shade tree near the pond. While aides returned to the ward for Calvin, she placed sunglasses on Petey, then sat back, quietly watching him.

"Waaa?" Petey asked.

"I'm looking at you. You're so very handsome."

Petey's eyes grew stern. "Oooo, oooo!" he grunted.

Cassie took his hand. "Petey, you are unlike any patient I have ever known. If I close my eyes, I can hear you speaking clearly. I can actually see you standing tall without a bent neck, twisted legs, and a wheelchair. Even with my eyes open, you are a tall, handsome man, as handsome as any I have ever seen."

Petey searched Cassie's eyes for sarcasm but found none.

As they waited, Cassie set little Lisa on Petey's chest. Cooing and gurgling, the baby ran her pudgy fingers across Petey's bent face. Petey cooed back with a high-pitched squeak. Lisa reached out and her tiny fingers grasped his ear. Smiling, Petey stared in wonder at Lisa's delicate, small, and perfect features.

As the attendants wheeled Calvin next to Petey, the band struck up a lively march. The drums and horns echoed brilliantly like laughter in the air.

"Pfer guuu! Pfer guuu!" Petey exclaimed.

"It sure is," Cassie grinned, taking Lisa back into her arms.

Petey and Calvin listened to the happy music made by young men and women in their colorful uniforms. Petey scanned the grounds, absorbing every detail. Ducks floated on the pond, propelled magically about. Squirrels chased each other through the trees, chattering over the strains of music. Rows of wooden benches lined the lawn, holding several hundred patients, most on good behavior.

At one point a loud roar drowned out the music. Petey traced the sound to a large machine actually flying through the air. The world was all magic, and he was alive!

For two glorious hours the band played. Cassie rested her hand on Petey's, bringing envious glances from Calvin. Because of her touch, Petey remembered precious little of the band's performance. By the time they returned inside, Calvin was laughing and making clown faces.

His good spirits did not go unnoticed. The next day, Cassie came up to Petey. "Petey, yesterday Calvin laughed for the first time. Did you see him?"

Petey smiled and grunted.

"I've been thinking. What Calvin needs in life is purpose. All people need purpose. Would you let Calvin be responsible for taking care of you?"

The thought made Petey nervous.

Cassie saw his concern. "It would make him feel needed. It's the best thing you could ever do for him."

Reluctantly, Petey agreed. That day it became Calvin's responsibility to get Petey around the ward and to let the attendants know when he needed changing. Helping to feed Petey was also part of Calvin's chores. Carefully he leaned over from his own wheelchair at mealtime and spoon-fed his reclined friend.

Calvin discovered it was great fun seeing if Petey could keep up with the spoon. Cassie reminded him to slow down, but one day while she was preoccupied at the other end of the table, Calvin shoveled large spoonfuls of mashed potatoes into Petey's gaping mouth. When Petey could not keep up, potatoes started piling up on his face. Laughing, Calvin reached over with his spoon, stealing food from other patients' plates. Unable to shake the globs of potato off his face, Petey sputtered with dismay.

By the time Cassie heard the laughing and choking, Calvin had nearly covered Petey's face. Other patients howled with laughter. Cassie ran over and scooped the potatoes off Petey's consternated face. Stifling laughter, she scolded Calvin.

Petey knew all that he endured helped to give Calvin purpose, but Cassie had said that *all* people needed purpose. If so, what was *his* purpose? What was Petey Corbin's reason for living? Was it to eat ground foods every day and mess his pads? That wasn't purposeful!

The thought haunted Petey.

Fresh memories of the world that existed beyond the ward made it fun to dream again. And there was Cassie—beautiful, enchanting Cassie. Two more times before summer ended, Cassie took Petey and Calvin outside. The last time, they stayed out so long that their skin turned bright red for almost a week and burned as if on fire.

Cassie fussed over them, blaming herself. She rubbed ointment on their faces and arms with strong gentle hands. Petey would have gladly been burned again if it meant getting to go outside and once more having Cassie run her hands across his arms and face.

Many evenings Cassie visited the ward and shared letters from her husband. One night in mid-October she stopped by, dressed in a long yellow cotton dress that made her seem more like an angel than an employee on an insane ward.

"Aaooo."

"Hello, Petey, how are you?"

"Pfer guuu." Petey sensed something different about this visit.

"Before we visit, do you need changing?" Cassie asked.

"Oooo, oooo." He lied. The nurses and attendants could clean him later—not Cassie, his friend, who stood beside him smiling with dimpled cheeks. Again the feeling came back to him. Something was different about this visit. "Waaaee, waaaee?"

"Why am I visiting you?"

"Aeee, aeee."

"'Cause you're such a handsome cuss, that's why."

"Guuu baa." Petey used the term as a good natured version of "Oh, go on." Cassie's smile brought a warm rush over his body that spread into his frozen limbs.

"No, really, Petey, you are handsome. Have you ever looked in a mirror?"

"Oooo."

"Well, hold your jolly horses, I'll be right back." Cassie disappeared briefly to the nurses' station. Petey's gaze escorted her. She returned with a small, square mirror which she held up in front of him. "Look, Petey, now tell me you're not a handsome man."

Petey gazed at the mirror, his eyes moving back and forth across the image. He saw someone with short, dark hair, a large nose, squared jawbones, and a lean, angular face. He puckered his cheeks and watched the image do likewise. Next he rolled his swollen tongue around his mouth, eyes intent on the mirror. Twisting his head about, Petey stared in utter fascination at his reflection.

"See, I told you," Cassie teased.

"Guuu baa." Petey felt she was stalling, so he caught her eyes once more. "Waaa?"

Cassie set the mirror slowly on Petey's night-stand and looked down, not answering for a moment. "Petey, I got a letter today from Alex. He's coming home."

"Guuu, guuu, guuu."

"Yeah, it's good, but it means I'm leaving here."

Cassie's words hung menacingly in the air. It wasn't possible. Cassie leaving? "Waaaee?"

"Petey, Alex is flying into New York, and I'm leaving tomorrow to meet him."

"Kkaa bak," Petey pleaded.

As Cassie looked down, she was crying. The gentle curve of her cheek trembled, and the little dimples had vanished. "No, Petey, I can't come back. New York is a long, long way from here, and Alex will be stationed there. I won't lie to you, Petey, and say something that's not true. You're too good a friend."

Petey saw tears flowing from Cassie's eyes. He was scared—scared she was leaving, scared he had done something terrible to make her cry. He was just a hideous and grotesque patient in an insane ward. He was someone without purpose and without a family, this he knew. She shouldn't miss him. She shouldn't cry.

"Oooo, amm oooo guuu, amm oooo guuu." Petey wailed.

"No, no, you *are* good."

"Oooo, oooo."

"Petey." Cassie reached down and lifted his hand, her big, almond-colored eyes glistening with tears. "Don't ever think you're no good. You're a wonderful person."

"Oooo, oooo." Petey forced his words out, irritation in his voice over such a preposterous statement.

"I mean it with all my heart." Cassie lifted his arm and held it tightly against her breasts.

"Oooo, oooo." Petey tried to pull his arm down, but she pressed her cheek against his crooked hand. Petey could feel her warm tears wet his fingers. His jaw quivered. He had caused Cassie to cry. Now his heart beat so hard he was sure she could hear it.

"Petey, listen to me. You're the most remarkable person I've ever met. You've never been selfish or mean, not once. You're always concerned about my problems, or wanting to know how Calvin or Lisa is doing."

"Amm oooo guuu!"

She squeezed his limp, motionless hand tightly. "Damn it, yes you are! This body and this wheelchair isn't *you*. You're a knight in shining armor. You're brave and wonderful, and I love you." Her voice trembled.

Petey had lost his will to struggle against this woman he adored. Tears swelled in his eyes. As Cassie cried above him, Petey sensed a softness and vulnerability in her. He wanted to hold her, to protect and comfort her in his arms. He damned the forces that froze his body and kept him from reaching out to this woman who at this moment needed his touch, his embrace.

"Aaaa ufff uuu! Aaaa ufff uuu!" Petey cried, tears dripping from the sides of his eyes.

They gazed at each other with tear-streaked faces. Cassie lowered his arm to her waist. "I love you, too, Petey, very, very much," she whispered. Bending over, she brought her face close to his.

Raw fear struck at Petey. Something was happening that he didn't understand, that he couldn't control. Gently, ignoring his fear, Cassie pressed her lips against his cheek. For the first time Petey truly believed how sincerely she felt. The realization tore at his heart.

As she pulled away, Petey panicked—it could not end like this. It would never be right unless he had done the same. Puckering his lips in a circle, he grunted. Cassie understood his gesture. Once more she lowered her head. This time she pressed her soft cheek gently against his distorted lips. For a long, precious moment she allowed Petey to complete their contract of emotion.

Then Cassie stood and slipped a fine, long chain around his neck. On it hung the golden half of a broken heart. The other half she wore around her own neck.

"Petey, on the front of these little pieces of heart it says, 'May the Lord watch between me and thee while we are absent one from the other.' On the back it says, 'We shall remember.' That means that if ever you're lonely, just remember me and I'll be thinking of you. And if ever I'm lonely, I'll remember you and know you're thinking of me. We can't be sad, though. Many people live their whole lives not knowing love. You and I have been lucky."

Petey choked back mighty sobs. "Aeee, aeee."

"Good-bye, Petey."

"Guuu baa, Keessee, guuu baa."

Cassie blurred as she walked away. She was his family, his love, a shimmering angel walking out of his life and taking heaven with her. For almost an hour he mouthed the words, "Aaaa ufff uuu, aaaa ufff uuu, aaaa ufff uuu." Tears flowed from some endless reservoir.

Chapter 12

1965 (twenty years later)

After Cassie left, the relentless passage of time within the brick walls of Warm Springs had continued unabated. As people escaped civilization to enjoy the solitude of a mountain peak, so also did many of the patients' minds escape existence and find solitude beyond the reaches of the ward. Some fled to places from which they could never return.

For Petey, whose thoughts remained inside the ward, the rhythm of monotony etched ever deeper into his mind as if chiseled in stone. But for Calvin, the rhythm grew obscure. His mind began taking leave.

Nothing changed this relentless pattern until a rusted yellow Chevrolet pulled slowly off the highway and through the front gate of Warm Springs in the spring of 1965. Inside sat a bespectacled, thin man whose weathered and callused ranch hands looked crowded by his suit coat.

"Not exactly Palm Beach," Owen Marsh grunted, wondering if it was a mistake to have come here instead of retiring. He had wanted to do something to help people. This was the only facility willing to hire someone over sixty-five years old.

He examined the paved streets lined with trees and imposing brick buildings. Ducks floated peacefully on a large, mirrored pond. Owen glided his dirty sedan to a stop in front of the administration building. Although now called a state hospital, it wasn't hard to imagine the place as an insane asylum.

As Owen entered the building, his tall, lean frame and silver-splashed hair made him look like a weathered professor. Muffled screams and shouts echoed ominously from cavernous hallways.

"State hospital, huh?" he mumbled, glancing around anxiously.

Within an hour, paperwork was finished and Owen reported to Ward 18 at the men's compound for orientation. A large, oafish attendant greeted him in the parking lot with, "Great! Now they send me fossils. Shouldn't you be retired?"

Owen smiled lightly. "Beats trying to shoot par at some golf course."

The attendant, whose nostrils sprouted little clumps of hair, shrugged. "To each his own." He extended his hand. "I'm Gus." He gripped Owen's bony hand.

"When do we start work?" Owen asked, smiling and returning a grip he had used to pull hundreds of calves during calving.

The attendant winced and jerked his hand free. Laughing weakly, he studied the new arrival. "How about now?" he offered, heading inside the building and up a steep stairwell. "Welcome to Ward 18. We don't put up with much in this zoo. If someone's too violent, too crazy, too anything, they get locked up." He chuckled. "Not that we don't have our share of goofballs. I'll introduce you to a few."

As the talkative, dough-faced attendant climbed the stairs, his frayed shoelaces dragged behind his dirty sneakers. His white shirt and pants were stained and faded. Big rolls of fat on his waist bounced like inner tubes, straining the buttons on his tight shirt. Reaching the second-floor landing, Gus breathed heavily.

As they entered the ward, thick cigarette smoke and a rank smell made Owen cringe. Country music blared from the room, mixed with screams and shouts. Strewn about the ward was every imaginable human oddity: tall and short, fat and thin, old, young, active, bedridden, many with "thousand-mile" gazes. Some wandered about like drunks leaning forward into unfelt wind.

"Hey, Gus," a voice bellowed from across the room. "Is he an attendant or one of us?"

Gus looked at Owen. "Which are you?"

Owen smiled weakly. "I'll start out as an attendant. Maybe later I'll join 'em."

"Won't be the first if you do."

Owen couldn't tell if Gus was serious. "First, I'll introduce you to Harold," Gus said as they approached the nearest patient. "Harold got smacked by a falling tree while logging over in the Bitterroots. How you doing, Harold?" Gus clapped the man on the back.

The stout man responded with a lifeless stare that followed them as they continued.

The next patient sat stiffly in a chair and smiled politely to them. "This is Cooper Elliot. Used to be a district judge until something snapped. He remembers every case he ever had, but can't recognize his wife and children. He don't even remember his own name."

After several more introductions, they approached the dayroom. Two long, wooden tables with stout benches divided the large glassed-off area. A TV against the wall scrolled its fuzzy black-and-white picture constantly upward. The assembled patients didn't seem to mind as they picked at their noses or swatted flies. At the far end of one table sat five men appearing quite normal. They joked, played cards, and smoked. Turning to leave, Owen stopped Gus. "How about those guys? What's with them?"

Gus motioned Owen to step outside the dayroom. Once clear he whispered, "They're criminals who beat legal raps with insanity pleas."

"They're normal?"

"It's what makes them dangerous. Steer clear of 'em."

Owen fought the urge to turn and run, but more odd sights waited in the far corner of the ward. A rotund, middle-aged man sat slumped over the arm of his wheelchair, his head and tousled hair draped against a bedridden patient. The patient in bed had severe deformities. Both appeared to be asleep.

"That one sitting in the wheelchair is Calvin Anders. He doesn't do nothin' 'cept eat, sleep, and crap. His mind is visiting China."

"How about the guy in bed?" Owen asked.

"That's Petey Corbin. He's an idiot retard, but a friendly one—you know, laughs and smiles a lot. Sometimes you swear he's thinking, but it's just conditioning. They used to get him up every day and put him in a wheelchair. Lucky for us, they stopped that."

"Must be friends," Owen commented, staring at the two odd men sleeping amidst the madhouse of noise. They looked to be in their late forties. He couldn't imagine forty years in this place.

"Yeah. Every day they're like this. When Calvin says something, Petey grunts back gibberish. Get used to these clowns, we got a bunch more of 'em. Any questions?"

"No, I guess not."

"Good, you've completed orientation. Let's work."

And work they did. Owen spent most of the afternoon helping bathe and dress nearly two dozen patients. The bathroom was stark, consisting of three rust-stained toilets without seats or covers and three equally stained and chipped ceramic wash basins. In a small room adjacent to the bathroom sat an old, clawfoot bathtub.

Not a smoker himself, Owen drew curses from several patients for not knowing how to roll cigarettes. Twice he stopped altercations by taking the patients aside and reasoning with them. He wondered how soon he might need more than diplomacy. Midafternoon, he found out.

"Hey, Owen, help me!" screamed Gus.

Owen turned to find Gus on the floor grappling with a burly patient. The two crashed against one of the sturdy metal beds. "Grab his arms!" yelled Gus.

Owen dove into the fray. Struggling, he discovered firsthand the strength and wildness of a psychotic patient. When they finally had the patient captive on a bed, with leather straps holding his arms and legs, Owen looked at Gus. "What started all this?"

"The jerk wouldn't take a bath."

"Did you try talking to him?"

"Sure. Told him if he wasn't undressed in two minutes I'd undress him."

Owen returned quietly to his work.

Late that afternoon while cleaning the deformed patient named Petey, Owen found himself looking for lotion. Opening the nightstand, his eyes fell on a small gold pendant with no chain. Under it lay an old, framed Bible verse. The pendant was in the shape of a broken heart. Owen picked it up. On the front was inscribed "May the Lord watch between me and thee while we are absent one from the other." On the back was engraved "We shall remember."

Owen looked up to find the crippled patient

examining him. It didn't look to Owen like anyone had remembered this patient. Surely no one had watched over him. Owen returned the pendant to the nightstand and picked up the framed Bible verse. It was the one about mounting up on wings like eagles, running and not being weary. He blew dust off the faded print. Someone had scratched out the word eagles and written pigeons.

As he placed the frame back in the drawer, Owen noticed Petey still staring intently at him, skin ashen from lack of sun. The quizzical look in Petey's eyes was unmistakable.

Chapter 13

Work at a state hospital opened up a world beyond imagination. Owen Marsh couldn't accustom himself to the tragic and violent nature of many patients. How could such small glitches in a human body wreak such havoc on a life?

Every waking hour of every day, loud country-western music blared from the ward. Amid the pervasive bedlam, the most touching sight was that of the two patients Petey and Calvin, together in self-imposed seclusion. Calvin rebuffed all attempts at conversation. He isolated himself in a small world where he wanted no company except

Petey. As for Petey, his haunting and penetrating stare, his understanding and kind eyes, defied idiocy.

Owen's first summer and fall passed. On Christmas Eve, he sat alone in his small apartment beside a token tree with no lights. There were no gifts, only memories of grown children and a divorce years earlier. The evening brought reflection. Owen wondered what he had to show for his life. Was anyone in the world better off because Owen Marsh existed?

On impulse, Owen went to his kitchen. Deliberately he wrapped two small bundles of candy and headed out into the cold night. Overhead, a full moon glowed so brightly it should have had a pull-string. A meteor traced a brief line across the sky. Walking in the fresh, moonlit air reminded Owen of the ranch he had once owned. On nights like this he had relaxed on the back porch, planning the next day's chores. He looked up at the stars shimmering in the cold air. A state hospital was a world apart from the ranch, and yet they shared the same sky.

When Owen arrived at the ward, the lights were already out. Quietly he moved between the rows of beds. He set one brightly colored gift on Calvin's nightstand. The other gift he placed near Petey. Owen stared at the relaxed and childlike peacefulness in Petey's face. Could this patient really think? When the night refused to divulge that secret, Owen reluctantly left.

The next morning, on Christmas Day, Owen visited the ward early to help Petey and Calvin open their gifts. Already Calvin sat parked beside Petey's bed, and the two were jabbering excitedly back and forth.

"Petey, can I open your present?" Calvin begged.

"Aeee." Petey motioned with his eyes.

Calvin ripped open the small gift. Petey motioned for Calvin to take some of his candy as a gift.

"Ah, thanks, Petey," Calvin said. "You're the best friend I ever had." Calvin picked several pieces of candy from his own bag and laid them next to Petey. "Here, this is my gift to you."

Conditioning, my foot, Owen thought, watching the two aging men. They seemed like children, innocent and helpless in a world that controlled them. Something in their essence went beyond the physical. Could they be more than deformed castoffs from society?

Soon Calvin leaned against Petey and closed his eyes. Again their smiles faded. Owen felt a sudden sorrow and an even deeper resolve. He had come to Warm Springs instead of retiring so that he could do something worthwhile. Until now, he had done nothing more than help patients exist.

The following day Owen was scheduled to work the afternoon shift, so with feverish purpose he went about his morning's activities. First he stopped by the ward. Approaching Petey and Calvin, he sat down beside them. He knew Calvin would not talk to him, so he faced Petey. "Petey, do you understand what I'm saying?"

Petey stared at him without response.

Owen pleaded, "Petey, do you understand what I'm saying? Please answer if you do. It's important."

Slowly, hesitantly, Petey nodded.

"Can you say yes?"

"Aeee," Petey answered with a pinched sound.

"What's that mean?"

"Aeee, aeee."

Owen listened to the guttural squeal and shook his head. "I don't know what that means."

Again Petey deliberately made the sound. "Aeee, aeee." His lips strained to form the words.

"I'm sorry, Petey, I don't understand you."

Behind Owen, Calvin's exasperated voice blurted, "He said yes, you *moron*!"

Owen spun around to look at Calvin, but Calvin had already returned to looking at his lap.

"Thanks, Calvin," Owen grinned, turning back to Petey.

"Aeee," Petey squeaked again.

Owen smiled. "Petey, if I can find you a wheelchair, would you like to get up each day and move around the ward? Go sit by the window or watch TV? Maybe even go outside? Do you understand what I'm asking you?"

Petey nodded his head with short, jerky movements.

"Okay, let's see what I can do. If I'm worth my salt, you two will get more than Christmas candy."

Petey allowed a guarded smile. Calvin still stared at his knees.

Soon, Owen rushed toward the administration building. Reaching the nursing director's office, he knocked on the open door and looked in. "Mrs. Elgin, may I speak with you a moment?" He breathed heavily.

The elderly lady shuffled through a stack of papers as she glanced up. "I'm quite busy. What is it, Mr. Marsh?"

Owen entered the office. "Mrs. Elgin, I've worked at Warm Springs now for six months on Ward 18. In our ward we have the usual assortment of mentally disturbed—"

"I'm familiar with Ward 18," Mrs. Elgin said curtly.

Owen knew the director was all business: straightforward, hardworking, and not one to lock horns with—not if you valued your head. He cleared his throat nervously. "We have two patients on our ward capable of much more than their records might suggest. From watching them, I think they are quite aware of reality. One, named Petey Corbin, is diagnosed as severely retarded and kept in his bed. The other, Calvin Anders, is also considered retarded. He may be, but I suspect his most serious problem is his club feet and severe depression. Both men are literally rotting away in the corner of our ward."

The phone rang. "One moment, Mr. Marsh," said the director. Another five minutes passed. Several people poked their heads in the door to whisper messages or reminders. As she talked on the phone, Mrs. Elgin's hands and eyes moved constantly, jotting notes and signing forms. Finally the call ended. "I'm sorry, Mr. Marsh. We were talking about two patients. Tell me, if they appreciate reality, why is the one so withdrawn and depressed?"

"I'd be depressed, too, if twenty-four hours a day someone kept me trapped inside the raving chaos of an insane ward. Depression, in a way, proves sanity."

"I don't agree with your reasoning, Mr. Marsh, but let's assume you're right. How would you change their existence? These patients have no other place to go."

"I realize that, but I could open up their world.

I'd like to get Petey a wheelchair and plan some activities."

"What kind of activities?"

Owen didn't like how matter-of-fact her voice was. Nor did he want to get in a spitting match. "Movement about the ward to watch TV," he said calmly. "Day trips outside. Anything to offer hope and purpose. All anyone needs from life is hope and purpose."

Mrs. Elgin narrowed her eyes in an accusing stare. "And so, Mr. Marsh, what is your purpose here? Why are you so concerned with these two men?"

Owen looked down and paused for an uncomfortable moment. Again the phone rang. This time Mrs. Elgin picked up the receiver and asked the calling party if they could hold. She punched the hold button and cradled the phone in her hand, looking again at Owen. "Go ahead, Mr. Marsh. What is your purpose here?"

Owen glanced with dismay at the flashing light on the phone. "Mrs. Elgin, for months all I've done is help these two patients survive. In so doing, I've only existed myself. I need more—not just for them, but for myself."

"That's noble, Mr. Marsh. But we have limited resources. If a patient is diagnosed severely retarded, it is not your position to question that. Patients are reevaluated regularly by trained doctors and psychologists. If a patient can be helped, services are available, including physical and occupational therapy."

Owen gripped the sides of his chair tightly. "That isn't enough—more needs to be done for Petey."

"I'm not familiar with his case, Mr. Marsh, but considering his diagnosis, that level of existence is not unusual. As for this Calvin patient—he's afforded the same opportunities as other patients. Provided he's not violent, he's free to watch TV or attend the dances and movies we provide here on the grounds. How he responds to opportunities, however, is up to him. I'm sorry but I will not authorize special privileges for these individuals."

"Do you mind if I spend my own time helping them?" Owen asked bluntly.

Mrs. Elgin gave Owen an icy stare. "I can't dictate how you spend your free time. It's not good practice, however, to become involved with patients. Now, if you will please excuse me, Mr. Marsh, I'm very busy." She lifted the phone to her ear.

Owen stared at the woman, his face flushed with anger. He stood and walked slowly from the room.

After his conversation with Mrs. Elgin, Owen stewed. Her logic was so wrong. Deliberately, he rebelled. Each day he smuggled in chocolate bars and spent extra time with Petey and Calvin.

Petey relished the chocolate bits placed in his mouth. His coiled tongue smeared chocolate against his gums and his few remaining teeth— Owen suspected Petey's teeth had been pulled out one at a time as they rotted. Calvin refused candy directly. Eyeing the chocolate Owen left next to his bed, he waited until he was alone, then devoured it greedily. Sometimes he stuffed whole bars into his mouth, looking like a chipmunk.

With time, Owen learned Petey's sounds and gestures and grew more fond of the deformed man. Calvin proved more difficult. His depression locked him in a lethargic apathy. Owen wondered what key could ever open Calvin's closed world.

Owen knew that blatant disobedience might cost him his job, but how else could he get Petey out of bed? One day an old, wooden-seated wheelchair remained on the ward after a patient transfer. Immediately Owen rolled it over to Petey. "Hey, sport, you ready to get out of bed?"

"Aeee, aeee," Petey squeaked, grinning broadly.

"Okay, let's see if this works." With help from a sympathetic nurse, Owen lifted Petey into the chair. Petey grimaced, his body awkwardly bridging the upright contour of the old chair. "It needs changes, Petey," Owen allowed.

Knowing full well that what he planned could be considered destruction of state property, and doubting that Mrs. Elgin would approve the cost, Owen hauled the wheelchair into the nearby town of Anaconda on his day off. Cutting and bending, a welder modified the back into a reclining position and extended the seat straight out to hold Petey's contracted legs. To all of this Owen taped a good deal of padding. That afternoon, he wheeled the modified chair into the ward. "What do you think, Petey?"

Petey stared at the contraption, his anticipation and doubt both evident.

"Let's go for a spin," Owen coaxed.

Petey needed no coaxing. "Aeee, aeee."

Owen placed a pad and two pillows on the chair. A nurse helped swing Petey into place. "How is it?" Owen asked.

Petey strained and wiggled, then relaxed, letting his body settle in. "Guuu, guuu." Delight showed in his eyes.

"Okay, drive carefully."

Petey smiled. "Ohhh guuu baa." He twisted his neck in every direction, straining to look about.

"Where do you want to go first?"

Petey motioned with his eyes toward the windows. As Owen positioned him, Petey squinted out at his small square allotment of the world beyond walls. His eyes darted about as if the view might be taken from him. "Aeee, aeee," he squealed.

Owen couldn't imagine what it would be like to look outside for the first time in years. For half an hour Petey feasted his eyes on the trees, the grass, the sunlight, absorbing the meager view as if nothing could ever fully saturate his starved senses. At mealtime, Petey begrudgingly left his post at the window.

"You'll get to do this every day," Owen promised.

Doubt showed in Petey's eyes.

Owen dreaded a visit from the director of nursing, but one day Mrs. Elgin appeared unexpectedly and discovered Owen rolling Petey across the ward.

"Good day, Mr. Marsh," she said, eyeing Petey and his modified chair. "Is this one of the patients you discussed with me?"

Owen drew in a deep breath. "Yes. Let me introduce you to Petey Corbin. Petey, this is Mrs. Elgin."

"Aaooo, aaooo."

"He's saying hello," Owen interjected.

Mrs. Elgin eyed Petey, then Owen, and then Petey's modified wheelchair. Owen thought he detected a slight smile.

"Hello, Petey. Do you enjoy your wheelchair?" she asked.

"Guuu, guuu."

"He says good, Mrs. Elgin."

"So he does." Mrs. Elgin faced Owen. "You're a very determined person, aren't you, Mr. Marsh?"

Owen nodded.

"Well, I must be getting on. I'm sure I'll be speaking to you again . . . and you, too, Petey. Good day."

"Guuu baa."

Mrs. Elgin held up her hand to Owen. "I know Mr. Marsh . . . don't tell me. That's goodbye."

Petey smiled broadly. "Aeee, aeee."

Owen smiled. He suspected his next talk with Mrs. Elgin would not be the reprimand he had feared.

Chapter 14

After Mrs. Elgin's visit, Owen organized more activities for Petey and Calvin. Each Friday night he took them to watch a movie. Each Wednesday night he visited the ward on his own time and took both men dancing.

Dances held in the Warren Building were lively events, with a band made up entirely of patients. Several of the band members had been concert musicians before coming to Warm Springs, and although unstable, they retained their musical abilities.

Owen would wheel Petey out on the dance

floor and move him back and forth to the sound of waltzes and fox-trots. During these moments, Petey tilted his head back and closed his eyes. A blissful smile betrayed his thoughts.

Trips to movies or dances meant going outside. Calvin never showed any reaction, but Petey opened up with intense laughter and wonderment. Rolling down the sidewalk, he cooed contentedly.

Daily, Owen tried to keep his two friends entertained. Ignoring the protests of other patients, he allowed the two men to watch their favorite TV shows. Unable to say Calvin's name, Petey adopted the name "Ike" after watching a documentary on Dwight Eisenhower. This was a name he could pronounce without using his tongue. Soon Petey called, "Ieeekk! Ieeekk!"

Petey's favorite shows were *Wagon Train* and *Have Gun Will Travel*. *The Three Stooges* helped Calvin venture from his self-imposed exile. One day after watching *The Three Stooges*, Calvin picked up a broom and swung it in circles. Accidently he whacked Petey in the face and knocked out three of his teeth. For the next month, Petey grunted at

Calvin to keep away. Only after dozens of apologies did Petey finally allow Calvin near.

Life continued playing hardball with Petey. Being spastic, he often suffered damage from uncontrolled jerks. One day while being shaved with a straight-edged razor, a noise surprised him. The resulting jerk opened up a four-inch gash across his right cheek.

Nearly two years after Owen befriended him, Calvin began opening up his closely guarded world.

"Calvin," Owen asked one day, "what did you think about when you were lying each day by Petey's bed?"

"I was dreaming. I seen people go crazy in this place with all the noise and stuff. Only way I could get away from it was to dream. Mostly about castles and dungeons, you know, 'cause they have people screaming in dungeons."

"Ever dream about anything else?"

Calvin blushed. "Well, yeah. Sometimes about pretty girls. That way I wouldn't go nuts."

Owen laughed. "That would *drive* me nuts."

Calvin smiled big. "Maybe we're both crazy."

"Yeah, maybe you're right," Owen agreed.

By 1973 Owen knew he must leave Warm Springs. The daily regimen demanded too much. Stricter rules and directives from a new administrator hastened his decision. One week a newly posted notice forbade the feeding of bread and crackers to the ducks on the pond. Evidently patients were saving food and feeding their feathered friends. Owen shook his head in disgust. How could such a simple pleasure be taken from people already so deprived?

Owen made up a papier-mâché duck. The morning he left, he defiantly floated it on the pond. He hung a sign around the duck's neck that read, "Give us this day our daily bread." Owen laughed as he left the pond, but his amusement had disappeared by the time he entered the ward to bid his friends good-bye. Chatting, he wandered among the staff and patients, shaking hands with each of them. After nearly an hour, the duty nurse chided him, "Owen, either leave or get back to work."

Owen smiled sadly. "I still have to talk to Petey,"

he said. He had been avoiding this painful task. He wasn't worried about Petey's care. Now Petey had become everybody's favorite patient. Someone had even started a photo album for him. Several of the nurses fussed over him and Calvin as if they were children. No, what Owen dreaded was his own loss. Petey had almost become family.

Petey loved life more than any human Owen had ever met. Petey savored moments with fathomless appreciation. Simple joys and pleasures became splendid happenings. His compassion and thoughtfulness defied reason.

Owen spotted Petey sitting near an open window, absorbed in thought. "Beautiful day," he remarked.

Petey started, jerking his arms wildly. "Aeee. Waa?" He knew this was Owen's day off.

"Petey, I'm afraid I have some bad news."

"Waa, waa?" Petey's arms jerked again, straining with the question. Concern clouded his eyes.

"I'm leaving Warm Springs."

Petey sat stunned. "Waaaee."

"'Cause I'm getting to be an old duff now. I'm seventy-three. It's time they put me out to pasture."

Disbelief muddled Petey's gaze. "Uuu oooo gooo!"

"I have to go, old buddy. I'll be staying in Montana, so I'll visit." Owen turned away from Petey's agonized gaze. Staring down, he struggled with his words. "I want you to remember something for me, will you?"

"Waa?" Petey grunted, his grief evident.

"Someday, somewhere, there's gonna be a better world. When we get there, my friend, you're gonna be at the front of the line. You hear me, the front of the line." Owen leaned over, giving Petey a strong hug.

Petey hugged back, using only his emotions.

After Owen left, Petey withdrew into himself. Owen visited only once. The visit devastated Petey, as well as Calvin, reminding them of their loss. Petey resigned himself to the empty feeling. He had many friends at Warm Springs, but they weren't the same as Owen. Now Petey felt old. He could not recall how old he was but he knew he was well over fifty.

Petey suspected that the numbing rhythm of time

that permeated his existence would be the rhythm that carried him into eternity. He accepted life and the metronome of boredom as he did his twisted limbs. He accepted not having a family, and he resolved to no longer allow hope to torment him with empty promises. This resolve gave Petey a certain feeling of control.

That feeling, however, did not last. In the fall of 1975, Petey noticed patients being moved from the ward. The Christmas of 1977, Calvin was taken away without warning. The only explanation given was that he had been transferred. One month later, a nurse announced, "Petey, tomorrow you're moving to Bozeman."

"Waaaee?"

"As part of a state modernization program, anyone who can be better cared for elsewhere is being moved out. You'll do better in a nursing home."

Petey's mind raced. He had never known any place other than Warm Springs. What was a nursing home?

The nurse saw his fear. "Don't be scared. You're going to a place called Bozeman Nursing Home. It's a nice place without all the noise and crazy people. You'll have your very own TV and you'll get to go outside. Each month you can buy things you want. You'll make wonderful new friends."

Petey shook his head forcefully. Everything he knew and understood was here. The unknown frightened him terribly. Why couldn't he stay at Warm Springs and have Calvin back?

"Hhoo ba Ieeekk?" he blurted, forcing his words out frantically. "Hhoo ba Ieeekk?"

The nurse shook her head and gave Petey an apologetic look as she turned to leave. "I'm sorry, Petey, I just don't understand you."

After she left, Petey couldn't shake the haunting question in his mind. How about Ike? That evening a bleak wind blew down across the hospital grounds, wrapping Petey tightly in despair. He felt as bitter as the wind. Where was Calvin tonight? Was he okay? They had never even gotten to say good-bye to each other.

Late into the night the wind howled loudly, keeping Petey awake. Warm Springs was all he'd ever known, all he ever wanted, and all he could imagine. Everything in his universe was visible from the ward. Where was Bozeman, and how would he get there? He was in a wheelchair! What did they do with people in wheelchairs?

The following morning, Petey hid behind a deep silence as a nurse prepared him for leaving. "Petey, today's the big day. You're going on a train ride," she said. "In Bozeman, they'll pick us up at the depot. I'll go with you to the nursing home. Aren't you excited?"

Petey closed his eyes tightly, but the darkness refused to dissolve his fear.

Soon the noise of the train pounded Petey with a rhythmic *click-clack, click-clack.* The sound had a vague and haunting familiarity. Crazed with fear—like a frightened rabbit—Petey wanted to run and never stop.

As the train screeched to a halt in Bozeman, snowflakes as big as quarters drifted down, silhouetting the brick depot. A white van pulled into the yard, swung a large arc in the lot, then backed against the dock. Nobody, including Petey, could see the ghost of a little boy carried onto a train at this very spot half a century earlier.

Inside the van, Petey closed his eyes and shuddered deeply. Not until they rolled him into Bozeman Nursing Home did he open his eyes. He rebuffed any smiles and encouragement as he lay helpless, his worst nightmare becoming real.

As curiosity gradually chipped away at Petey's fear, he felt himself pulled into a cramped little room. Without help, a grated door closed. The movement startled Petey, and his arm struck the wall hard. He stared through the grating in confusion. The whole room was moving downward.

"Hey, Petey," the nurse chimed, "I'll bet this is your first ride in an elevator, isn't it?"

Petey refused to speak as they wheeled him into a small corner room, barely large enough for his bed, a chair, and his wheelchair. He did notice it had windows—big, open, wonderful windows that covered two whole walls.

An hour later, as the nurse from Warm Springs prepared to leave, Petey broke his silence. "Guuu baa, guuu baa," he blurted desperately to the last departing shred of his world. And then he was totally alone. Nurses and aides kept entering the room to meet Petey, each failing to hide surprise.

Seeing his twisted features, they administered looks of sympathy then hastily exited.

Bozeman Nursing Home and Warm Springs shared the same rhythm of life—slow, methodical, monotonous. The first weeks were pure hell. Nurses and aides meant well but picked Petey up awkwardly, sending searing pain through his legs and back. Unaware that he wanted coffee, aides ignored his gestures and grunts. Instead of letting him cough himself out of choking spells, they pulled him forward and clapped his back, making matters worse. Several nights they placed him on his back to sleep. Moronic stares met his attempts to move. Unable to change position, he was tormented through the night.

Hating to show irritation or anger, Petey had to force his will simply to survive. Pinched screams and icy stares helped communicate his displeasure.

And he was lonely. The memory of Calvin came back to haunt Petey. Where had he been taken? Calvin became a simple memory of another time and another place. He no longer really existed.

Life around the nursing home became a schedule

that Petey lived by. Breakfast, lunch, and supper. Thursday he played Bingo—a volunteer moved his chips for him. Friday mornings, sing-along. Sunday, church services. With the coming of spring, aides placed Petey on the front lawn each day to enjoy the sun. He loved the school buses that roared past, carrying students home from a nearby school.

Nothing, however, warded off the bitterness that enveloped Petey. Now he knew how Calvin had felt all those years, alone and afraid. Petey knew he could control his happiness by thinking of only good things, but why was it that every time he loved something, it left? First there had been Esteban. Next it was the mice. Then Joe, and Cassie. . . . He would never forget Cassie. After that, Owen left. Then he had lost Calvin.

They were *his* family, the only family he'd ever known. He still loved them, and no one could replace them. No one! Parked alone on the grass one day, Petey made a vow. He would still be happy, but from now on, no matter how difficult, he would never allow himself to love anyone again. He had been hurt for the last time!

part two

Chapter 15

Spring 1990, Bozeman, Montana
(thirteen years later)

Trevor Ladd kicked at the wet spring snow as he walked home from school. Students shouted and laughed, throwing slushy snowballs. The air held a carnival atmosphere. Slowly at first, then more loudly, one disturbing sound clashed with the rest. A strange, grunting squeal pried at the air.

Trevor crossed the street to investigate the sound. As he rounded the corner by the nursing home, he spotted three eighth-grade boys from his class at school hiding behind a big pine tree. He recognized the school bullies: Kenny, the stocky one; Bud, the kid who always had a smirk on his face; and the tall, lanky one called String. They were lobbing snowballs over the tree onto the nursing home lawn.

Their target was a patient stretched out on a reclining wheelchair. A white sheet covered his legs. Wet slush drenched the old man. Each time a snowball hit him with a thud, the patient flailed his shriveled, clawlike arms and screeched. His eyes pinched closed with pain.

"Hey, quit that!" Trevor shouted, breaking into a run. In seconds he stood like a sentry beside the deformed man.

"Great, now we have two targets!" Kenny laughed, as he flung the next snowball hard, hitting Trevor in the neck.

"Knock it off!" Trevor shouted.

"I'll knock your *head* off," cackled String, unleashing a bullet that exploded against the wheelchair. "You're a dead man!"

Trevor stood his ground, a human shield. Again and again snowballs pelted him hard. With snowballs raining in from three directions, Trevor did not see the hard-packed missile before it struck his face. Sharp pain pierced his eye as he bent over. "Help!" Trevor screamed at the top of his voice. "Somebody help!"

A fresh fusillade of snowballs rocketed in. Trevor laid himself over the old man and kept yelling. Suddenly the snowballs ceased. Trevor glanced up to see the three boys running down the street laughing.

"What's going on out here?" called a woman's voice.

Barely able to see with his right eye, Trevor saw a tall nurse rushing across the lawn toward them. "Get away from Petey!" she said, shoving Trevor away from the wheelchair. She brushed wet globs of snow off the patient.

"Oooo, oooo!" grunted the patient.

Trevor covered his watering eye. "Some guys were throwing snowballs at this old man."

"What guys?" the nurse asked sharply, fussing over the old man.

Trevor pointed up the street. "They're gone."

"What's wrong with your eye?" the nurse asked.

"I got hit," Trevor said, squinting.

The nurse, about the same age as Trevor's mom, turned to the man in the wheelchair. "Was somebody throwing snowballs at you?"

"Aeee, aeee," he squeaked.

"Did this boy throw them?"

"Oooo, oooo!" the shivering patient grunted, fear still wild in his eyes.

"Let's get you inside, Petey," said the nurse. She pointed at Trevor. "You come, too. What's your name?"

"Uh, Trevor Ladd."

"What were you doing out here?"

"Just walking home from school. I heard this squealing sound. Then I saw three boys throwing snowballs at this guy."

"Did you recognize the boys?" the nurse asked, wheeling the patient into the low, gray building.

"No," Trevor said, lying. The three bullies would kill anybody who squealed on them.

"You go to school here in Bozeman, and you don't recognize the boys?"

"We just moved to town," Trevor said, partly telling the truth. They had moved before Christmas.

The nurse eyed him skeptically, taking a pen and notepad from her pocket. "I want your name and phone number."

Trevor gave the information, then looked toward the deformed patient. "If you don't believe me, ask him." After a pause, he added, "If you can."

"Oh, I can. And I will. Now if you'll excuse me, I need to get Petey into something dry and warm. Things like this can kill an older person." She spoke accusingly.

As Trevor left, he glanced about. There was a faint, rotten smell. Patients sat everywhere, slumped in their chairs. Some stared at the ceiling. Others shook their heads or hands uncontrollably. Still others drooled. The place was a nuthouse of crazy old people, and Trevor couldn't leave fast enough.

When Trevor arrived home, his mom and dad were still working. They were always at work, it seemed. Trevor saw the postman more often than his parents. Today, Trevor was glad they weren't home. How could he explain what had happened without getting into more trouble? His parents might call the nursing home or maybe the bullies' parents.

Later that evening, however, Trevor couldn't hide his swollen eye. "What in the world happened to you?" his mother asked at supper.

"Got hit by a snowball," Trevor said weakly.

"You could lose an eye throwing snowballs," his father said severely.

"Yes, Dad," Trevor mumbled, thinking about the madhouse of crazy people he had seen that afternoon. Dozens of times he had walked past the nursing home without imagining the loony bin that existed inside. It was like an insane asylum.

At school the next day, Trevor tried to avoid the bullies, but Kenny cornered him in the hallway and shoved him hard against the lockers. "We're gonna get you," he growled, jabbing Trevor with a finger.

When school let out, Trevor avoided the bullies and the nursing home by several blocks. He didn't like old people much—most were weird. Not as weird, however, as the ones he'd seen yesterday. Throwing his jacket on the table when he arrived home, Trevor opened the refrigerator in search of a snack. As he ate a sandwich, he listened to the messages on the answering machine.

All the messages were for his parents except one from the Bozeman Nursing Home. The nurse, Sissy Michael, had called, wanting to talk to him again. After making sure to erase the message,

Trevor hesitantly returned the call. Maybe the nurse still thought he had hurt the old man.

"Bozeman Nursing Home," answered a woman's voice.

"Hi, is Sissy Michael there? This is Trevor Ladd."

"Yes, this is Sissy. Thanks for calling back. First, let me apologize for how I treated you yesterday. After talking to Petey, it appears you did protect him."

"It's no big deal," Trevor said, wishing this whole thing would just go away.

"It *is* a big deal," Sissy said. "That's why I called. Yesterday Petey was too cold and scared to thank you. He asked if you would stop by."

"Uh, that's okay, just tell him I'm glad he's okay."

Sissy's voice grew more serious. "I'm sure this place is probably frightening if you've never been in a nursing home before, but it really would mean the world to Petey if he could say thanks in person. Will you stop by?"

"Uh, I suppose."

Before Trevor could think of another excuse, Sissy hung up. Trevor hit his forehead with his palm, suddenly afraid. Why had he agreed to go back inside that crazy place?

At supper, Trevor's mom said, "I called home earlier and listened to the phone messages on the machine. What was that call for you from the nursing home?"

Trevor caught his breath, then shrugged. "Some guys were throwing snowballs at an old man. They thought I might have been one of the guys."

Trevor's dad eyed him sternly. "Were you?"

"Yeah, right!" Trevor shoved back from the table. "You think I'd throw snowballs at an old person?" Trevor stomped out the front door. He might as well go to the nursing home and get his visit over with.

"Where are you going?" his mom called.

"To throw snowballs at old men!" Trevor shouted angrily. All of this had gotten too weird for him. Being accused of throwing snowballs couldn't have been any worse than visiting this nuthouse to speak to some deformed old geezer.

As Trevor approached the brick building, an old man kneeling beside the flower bed looked up and waved. The guy had long, shiny, silver hair and baggy coveralls. "Wanna help plant?" he called.

"Uh, I'm busy," Trevor said politely, glancing at the old man's work in the fresh soil. "What are you planting?"

"Cigarette butts," came the answer.

Sure enough. The man had a dozen little holes dug. In each he had carefully placed a cigarette butt. "Whaddya think?" he asked proudly.

Trevor ignored the question and rushed inside the building. The guy was nuts. This whole place was full of crazy people. He found Sissy Michael as quickly as he could.

"Hi, Trevor," Sissy said pleasantly. "I'll be right with you." Her smile was warm.

"I can come back later to see the patient," Trevor said, searching for any excuse to get out of the place.

"Oh, no. I'll just be a minute."

Trevor didn't have to wait long.

"Follow me," Sissy said, leading Trevor to the end of a long hallway and down two flights of stairs. As she walked, she spoke. "The people you see at this nursing home are residents, not patients. Patients are in hospitals. Some of these residents have the most incredible backgrounds. One lady was thrown off a covered wagon at the turn of the century simply because she was mentally retarded."

"Are you kidding?"

"Nope. Petey Corbin, the guy you helped yesterday, was born with cerebral palsy but misdiagnosed as a baby. Most of his life, people have treated him like an idiot."

"What's cerebral palsy?" Trevor asked.

"A nervous system disorder. Petey is mentally sharp, but his mind is locked inside a defective body. He's a very special person."

"What's so special about him?"

Sissy smiled. "His incredible appreciation for life even though life hasn't always been so good to him."

As they walked, Sissy kept stopping to visit with residents. She didn't treat the people like they were nuts. She would say things like, "Don't worry, Herman, the Russians won't bomb this place," or "Yes, Mabel, this is Wednesday. Tomorrow you play Bingo."

One skinny and wrinkled woman in a yellow, baggy dress teetered along, her arm reaching for help. "Right down there, Elizabeth," Sissy said, pointing. "Your room is just down the hall. Here, we'll help you. Trevor, maybe you could hold Elizabeth's arm so she doesn't fall."

Trevor hesitated. Just touching the gnarled old lady's frail arm might break it. She looked like a dried-up old weed. Nervously, as if handling fragile glass, Trevor held the bony appendage, turning to see if anybody was watching. What if she fell? Luckily he didn't have to find out.

After delivering Elizabeth to her room safely, Sissy stopped Trevor outside a doorway at the end of the hallway. She spoke in a hushed voice. "Trevor, you must remember this about Petey: he is not mentally retarded. Given a different body, he'd be standing and talking to us right now."

"So what's the big deal with my visit?"

"Thirteen years ago they transferred Petey here from Warm Springs State Hospital. Warm Springs used to be an insane asylum."

"You mean this guy grew up in an insane asylum?

Sissy Michael nodded. "Yes, I'm afraid so. Yet Petey has a capacity for happiness that nobody completely understands. Since coming here, though, he has not allowed himself to make any close friends. This morning when he made it clear he wanted to see you, it was the first I've seen him reach out to anyone. What you did yesterday meant a great deal to him."

Trevor nodded, wiping his sweaty hands against his pants. Why was he so scared? He was just meeting an old man—no big deal. Entering Petey Corbin's small room, Trevor held his breath.

Reclining backward, Petey looked ready to wheel into an operating room. The twisted shapes under his cover sheet made Trevor cringe. What kind of legs could form such shapes? Petey's thin arms bent awkwardly at the elbow, resting beside him with limp bird-claw hands. His tongue coiled strangely in his opened mouth, his head hunched sideways. He had a short gray beard and mustache. A long scar angled across his right cheek. Had somebody attacked this guy?

"Petey," Sissy said warmly, "this is Trevor Ladd. You two met yesterday."

Trevor hesitated, not knowing if he should shake Petey's lifeless hand. Awkwardly Trevor waved and stammered, "Hello, Petey, I'm glad to meet you."

Petey looked up curiously. "Aaooo."

Trevor looked to Sissy for help.

"Petey just said hello," she said.

"Hello, Petey. Sissy has told me about you."

Petey looked over at Sissy. "Waa? Waa?"

Sissy smiled. "Tell Petey what I've told you."

Trevor felt two penetrating eyes settle on him and trap him like prey. Petey's body might have been useless, but his eyes sure weren't. Standing motionless, Trevor sensed he should never lie to this man. "Well," he stammered, "Sissy said you were raised in an insane asylum." Trevor rushed his words nervously. "And that you can understand everything I say."

Petey nodded. He eyed Trevor's swollen eye and jutted out his chin in concern. "Ooooaaaee?" he asked.

"He asked if you're okay."

"Oh, yeah. It was nothing."

"Aaaauuu," Petey grunted.

"He's thanking you," Sissy said.

Trevor smiled nervously. "It's no big deal."

For several awkward moments, Petey and Trevor stared at each other. Fingering a shirt button, Trevor blurted, "I better go."

Again Petey gripped Trevor with his stare, grunting, "Uuuu viii?"

Trevor looked to Sissy again for help.

"He wants to know if you'll visit him."

Trevor squirmed and said, "Maybe," knowing there was no way he would ever come back. Trevor wanted out. Out from in front of Petey's wheelchair. Out from this nursing home and the crazy people living here. This place gave him the creeps. "Petey, I gotta go," Trevor stammered. "It was nice meeting you."

Disappointment showed clearly in Petey's eyes. It was obvious he knew Trevor had lied. He motioned with his chin. "Guuu baa." His good-bye seemed a command.

As they walked back upstairs, Trevor said quietly to Sissy, "I think he was mad at me."

"Trevor, Petey has no family. He's scared to make new friends."

"So?" Trevor said, knowing all too well how that felt. Every time his family moved, he felt like an outsider again. After leaving his last bunch of friends, he had promised himself never to make the effort again.

Sissy spoke deliberately. "Today Petey took a huge gamble and reached out to someone new. He failed."

Trevor stumbled with his words. "He didn't fail. . . . It's just that . . . cripes, all I did was try to stop some guys from throwing snowballs at him. That's no big deal."

Sissy smiled gently. "It's a big deal for a helpless person."

Helpless, my foot, Trevor thought. With those eyes, he could kill a crow at a hundred yards by staring.

"Will you be back?" Sissy asked, following Trevor to the door. "Petey loves going on walks, but usually we don't have enough staff to get him out. And you never know, you might learn something from Petey."

"Maybe," Trevor said, knowing it would sound bad if he just came out and said, "No!"

"Don't say maybe if you don't mean it," Sissy said firmly.

Trevor took an angry breath. "Okay, I'm not coming back here! Now are you happy?"

Chapter 16

W e're gonna get your old friend, you moron!"
taunted Kenny, pointing his finger.

"He's not my friend!" Trevor shouted back.

Kenny's laughter cackled like bursts of machine
gun fire down the school hallway. "That crippled
fossil is your true love!" he hooted.

"He is not," Trevor mumbled under his breath
as he headed for his math class. He wished he had
never seen the old man or protected him from
snowballs.

When school let out that afternoon, Trevor
paused on the front steps. All of last week he had

purposely avoided going near the nursing home. Now he was worried by Kenny's threat. Reluctantly he walked in that direction.

As Trevor neared the big gray building, he spotted Petey parked out on the front lawn in the sun. If the three bullies were going to hassle the old man, it would probably be right after school. Trevor sat down behind a hedge half a block away and began his watch.

Staring at the distant man in his wheelchair, Trevor shook his head. How could somebody locked inside their body ever be happy? Sissy had said Petey had no family. "Lots of people don't have much family," Trevor mumbled, kicking at the grass.

This whole thing was making Trevor mad. It wasn't fair that jerks like Kenny picked on someone who was helpless. It wasn't fair that someone should be born locked inside their body. Lots of things weren't fair. It wasn't fair having to move new places every few years so his parents could get better jobs, Trevor thought. That definitely wasn't fair.

*　　　*　　　*

Each day Kenny kept threatening to hurt Petey, so each day Trevor sat guard after school near the nursing home. He couldn't believe how the old man sat for hours without speaking to anybody. What would it be like to be trapped inside a body, not even able to scratch an itch? Trevor decided there was no way this Petey guy could be happy.

On Friday, after sitting for his normal hour near the shrub, Trevor paused before heading home. His parents wouldn't be home until much later. Maybe it wouldn't hurt just to say hello to Petey. Hesitantly, as if entering a prison, Trevor walked to Petey's side. "Hello, Petey, do you remember me?"

Startled, Petey jerked. His bent arm flailed sideways and punched Trevor squarely in the stomach.

Trevor gasped. "Hey, it's just me! You remember me?"

Slowly a thin smile exposed Petey's toothless gums.

"I just stopped to say hello."

"Aeee!" Petey squealed. He flopped his head sideways and motioned with his eyes down the street.

"Yeah, I just came from school."

"Oooo," Petey said, looking down the street at the hedge where Trevor had been sitting.

"Did you see me sitting by the hedge?" Trevor asked.

"Aeee, aeee!" Petey squealed, smiling.

"Well, what have we here?" said Sissy Michael, her sudden appearance surprising both Trevor and Petey. Once more Petey jerked and flailed his arm. This time Trevor jumped to keep from being hit.

"Geez, you scared me," Trevor said to Sissy. "Why does Petey jerk and swing his arms when he gets surprised?"

"Most people have a surprise or jerk response. If I came up behind you on a dark street and said, "Booooo!" you would jerk, but only until your body arrested the movement. Petey can't stop the jerk. His whole body kicks, twists, or swings as far as it possibly can in any direction." Sissy eyed Trevor. "Did you come to visit Petey?"

Trevor shrugged. "I was just walking by and thought I'd say hi, that's all."

Petey grunted and glanced down the street toward the hedge. He jutted his chin out hard.

Trevor knew he had been caught in another lie. "Well, I was sitting by that hedge for a while first."

"Ah, so that's what Petey has been trying to tell me," Sissy said. "Each day this week, Petey has motioned toward the hedge before I rolled him in for supper."

Trevor studied Petey. "You mean you saw me sitting there each day?"

Petey nodded. "Aeee." Then a puzzled look spread across his face. "Waaa? Waaa?"

Trevor looked to Sissy for help.

"He wants to know why."

Trevor looked at Petey's intense stare. "Boy, you don't miss anything do you?"

"Oooo," Petey said. "Waaa?"

"Those guys that threw snowballs at you have been threatening to hurt you again, so I've just been sitting guard, that's all."

"So you do know who threw the snowballs." Sissy's eyes were accusing.

"I can't tell on them or they'll kill me," Trevor said, looking down.

Petey motioned back toward the hedge. Again he asked, "Waaa?"

"Petey wants to know why you sat by the hedge instead of coming to talk with him."

Trevor didn't know what to say. Everything he did seemed wrong. Around this old guy things got all screwed up. First he had tried to protect the guy, and he was accused of hurting him. Now he had tried to guard Petey, and he felt like he had done something wrong sitting behind a hedge half a block away. Trevor was afraid to speak, fearing his next words might dig his grave deeper.

"Waaa?" Petey demanded.

Sissy's eyes held the same question.

Swallowing, Trevor avoided Petey's eyes. "I was afraid of the bullies . . . and of Petey," he added. He glanced over at the old and twisted man. Instead of a defiant stare, Trevor found a warm, understanding nod.

"Guuu," Petey grunted, a smile creasing his lips.

"It's good I was afraid of you?" Trevor asked.

"No," Sissy said. "He means it's good you were finally honest with him."

Trevor looked long and hard at Petey. "So how have you been?" Trevor asked.

"Guuu, guuu," grunted Petey.

"Hey, Trevor, are you in a hurry?" Sissy asked.

"Uh, I guess not," Trevor said. "My parents never get home till late."

"How would you like to take Petey for a walk?"

Trevor balked. "Uh, I've never done anything like that before."

Petey smiled broadly.

"It's easy," Sissy said. "Here." She reached down and released a lever locking each rubber tire. "Just be careful going off curbs or over bumps. This old chair has seen better days." She motioned. "Go ahead, try."

Carefully Trevor pushed the contraption forward. "What if I don't understand what Petey says?" he asked, attempting to end this foolish venture.

Sissy laughed. "He'll teach you."

Big help Sissy was, Trevor thought as he started down the street. He looked around as he walked. With luck, nobody from school would see him. More than anything, he was glad to be behind Petey, away from his prying eyes.

Several times Trevor asked Petey questions but

couldn't understand the grunted responses. Petey seemed lost in his own world—he closed his eyes as they walked, cooing softly as if he were absorbing the early spring air.

People driving past twisted their necks to stare. Trevor wanted to crawl into a big hole. What in the world was he doing walking along a city street pushing a stretcherlike wheelchair holding a bent old man?

Petey noticed every little sound or movement. A huge truck roared past, beeping its horn. Petey flung his arms from side to side, smiling and laughing. "Ohh booee! Ohh booee!" he squealed. His expression beamed so intensely, Trevor laughed. "That was sure loud and big, wasn't it?"

Trevor realized that Sissy was right—it didn't take much to make Petey happy. Trevor also realized that if he was ever to communicate with Petey, he would have to learn a new language. Lastly, he discovered that Petey's wheelchair was a pile of junk. He had to stop four times to pull the rubber tire back on the wheel. The frame was broken and threatened to collapse with each bump.

As they rounded the corner, Trevor heard a loud

laugh. He looked up to find Kenny, Bud, and String barely a hundred feet away, blocking the sidewalk.

"Well, look who it is," Bud yelled, "the fossil and the dork."

"Bring your old fossil friend here," String shouted.

"Yeah, bring him here. We didn't get to meet him last time. Ha, ha, ha," Kenny cackled.

Trevor considered his options. The bullies blocked the sidewalk. He could run, but that would leave Petey alone. And trying to push Petey anywhere fast in the old wheelchair was out of the question.

"We're in trouble, Petey," Trevor whispered.

Chapter 17

Trevor's thoughts raced as the three boys sauntered toward them. "Hey, Petey," he whispered.

Petey looked up, fear clouding his stare.

"Can you make a bunch of noise and flop your arms around if you need to?"

Petey nodded.

"Okay, do it if I nod my head. Okay?"

Petey grunted his agreement as the boys approached. String gave Trevor a shove. "So what happened to your old buddy here? Did a garbage truck hit him?"

"Leave him alone," Trevor said, regaining his balance.

"Maybe the old fossil needs a real push. You push him like a wimp." Kenny grabbed Petey's wheelchair and started to spin it in circles. Petey frantically looked to Trevor for help.

"Stop it!" Trevor grabbed the edge of the wheelchair and stopped its turning. "You're going to hurt him!"

"A little spinning won't hurt anyone unless you try to stop us," said Kenny.

Before the stocky boy could start spinning Petey in circles again, Trevor spoke calmly and deliberately. "Petey gets seizures when he's scared."

"Yeah, sure, and I can get cancer if I pick my nose," Kenny taunted.

"Get out of the way, you twerp!" growled Bud, giving Trevor a shove that sent him sprawling on the sidewalk. Trevor looked up at Petey for a brief second and nodded.

Kenny grabbed the chair and started spinning Petey in circles. Suddenly Petey began grunting and squealing. His arms thrashed about and his body convulsed.

"He's having a seizure! You're killing him!" screamed Trevor from the lawn.

String balked. "Quit it, Kenny. Maybe he *is* having a seizure."

"Aw, shut up, you chicken!" said Kenny, spinning Petey faster.

"I'm getting out of here," Bud said suddenly. The boy turned and ran.

String nodded. "Knock it off, Kenny. You're hurting the guy. We just wanted a little fun. . . ." The lanky boy turned and ran after Bud.

Finding himself alone, Kenny looked around nervously and let go of the spinning wheelchair. Petey continued grunting and squealing like a siren, his bent arms thrashing about. Kenny backed away. "I didn't hurt him. Why is he flopping around and making so much noise?"

Trevor kept a serious face. "He's dying!"

Fear flashed across Kenny's face. "I didn't do nothing!" he stammered as the wheelchair stopped.

Trevor pointed an accusing finger. "If he dies, you'll be arrested for murder. If he doesn't die, he could still be permanently injured."

Kenny kept backing away. Petey, weakened by his effort, calmed down.

"See, he's okay," Kenny shouted.

Trevor bent over Petey as if listening to his chest. "Play dead, Petey," he whispered. Suddenly Petey went limp, his arms dangling lifelessly over the edge of the chair. "Oh, no, he's dead!" Trevor said. He looked Kenny directly in the eyes. "And you killed him."

The big bully stared at the wheelchair, his mouth opening and closing like a fish out of water. He shook his head. "Oh, no! I didn't mean it! I . . ." Then suddenly he turned and ran.

Trevor looked down at Petey, who had large beads of sweat on his forehead. "You okay?" he asked.

Petey opened his eyes and nodded. Then suddenly he started laughing, loud, intense, belly-shaking laughs. Trevor, feeling the old man's complete joy, laughed himself. "That was some seizure," he chuckled. "You even had me worried."

Petey grinned. "Aeee! Aeee!" Then he jutted out his chin. "Uuuu."

"You want me to try a seizure?"

Petey smiled. "Aeee."

Trevor grinned. "Okay." With that he fell down on the lawn and flopped around, making guttural snorts and gasps. Soon both of them were laughing so hard that tears rolled down their cheeks.

When they could finally talk again, Petey looked up and said, "Thaaa uuu, Twaaa."

"Are you saying thank you?"

"Aeee. Thaaa uuu, Twaaa." Petey jutted out his chin.

"Does Twaaa mean Trevor?"

"Aeee, aeee, aeee." Petey smiled a big toothless grin. "Thaaa uuu, Twaaa."

"You're welcome." Trevor squeezed Petey's shoulder.

Petey wiggled and smiled broadly.

Slowly Trevor pushed the wheelchair back toward the nursing home. Two weeks ago he had never even met this old and twisted man. Now he felt as if he had found a friend.

The following week as they finished a walk, Trevor said lightly, "Petey, you're fun."

Petey's face turned serious. "Waaaee? Waaaee?"

"Why? Because you're so crazy." Trevor knew instantly his answer hadn't satisfied Petey.

Several days later when Trevor visited, Petey's eyes leveled on him with a piercing stare. "Waaaee? Waaaee?"

"Why what, Petey?"

Petey waited.

Trevor's mind raced. Why? He couldn't still be referring to their conversation on the last walk. "Do you mean why do I like visiting you?"

"Aeee, aeee." Petey had a serious look on his face. "Petey, it's like I said. You're always happy. Who else can I push around and tell bad jokes to without getting hit?"

"Ohhh, guuu baa." Petey said his "good-bye" with a smile, so it meant "Oh, go on."

Trevor was glad Petey didn't push the question. He wasn't sure what he'd have said.

One week later, Trevor showed up just to say hello. Instead of his customary smile, Petey met Trevor with the same intent gaze. "Waaaee, Twaaa? Waaaee?"

Trevor stood staring. "Are you still asking me why I like to visit you?"

"Aeee."

"You're not letting me out of that question, are you?"

"Oooo." Petey's face fell deathly sober.

Trevor swallowed hard. "Okay, Petey, can we go for a walk and talk about it?"

Petey nodded.

The eighth-grade boy and the seventy-year-old man discussed many things that afternoon. Trevor did the talking and Petey grunted his agreements, disagreements, or questions. They talked about life, about bullies, about hurt, and about friendship. The conversation was awkward, but Petey waited patiently.

"Petey, maybe it's not you who needs all the help."

"Whhuu?" Petey's look was gentle, as if he knew Trevor was beginning to understand. "Whhuu?" he repeated.

"It's me, too," Trevor said. "If I don't care about you, I'm like the bullies. I go through life not caring. After moving to Bozeman, I needed a friend as much as you did."

"Guuu, guuu." Petey nodded.

The walk home was quiet in a very good way. Before Trevor left that day, he faced Petey and looked directly into the eyes he had once feared. "Petey, did I answer your question, why I liked visiting you?"

"Guuu," Petey grunted, a warmth filling his eyes.

"Hey, Petey, I have an idea," Trevor blurted.

"Waaaaa?"

"Let's do something different instead of just going for walks. How about fishing or shopping?"

"Aeee, aeee. Booow."

"Both?"

"Aeee, aeee."

"Okay, we'll do both. Which one first?"

"Fiii." Petey smiled in anticipation.

"Petey, have you ever been fishing?"

"Oooo."

Trevor held his fist to his mouth like a micro-phone and spoke loudly like an announcer. "Tomorrow, ladies and gentlemen, the one, the only, Petey Corbin shall catch his first fish!"

Petey glowed with anticipation. As Trevor left that afternoon, he heard Petey repeating the words "Gooo fiii, gooo fiii, gooo fiii."

Chapter 18

The next day at school, Trevor was still angry at the bullies for what they had done. As soon as he saw Kenny in the hallway, Trevor marched directly up and poked at his chest with a finger. Fear flickered in Kenny's eyes.

"The man in the wheelchair almost died yesterday," Trevor said. "If you jerks even sneeze near Petey, I'm calling the police. You'll be charged with attempted murder!"

Kenny backed away, holding his hands up as if for protection. "Hey, we didn't mean to hurt him or nothing."

Trevor turned and left, waiting until he was out of sight before grinning.

After school, Trevor stopped by home and picked up fishing poles and dug worms from the back yard. He grabbed some duct tape in case he needed to fix Petey's wheelchair. When he reached the nursing home, Trevor told Sissy about his idea to go fishing.

"Great," Sissy said. "I'll help you get ready."

Trevor followed Sissy excitedly to Petey's room.

"I'll show you how to clean and change Petey in case you ever have to help him on an outing."

"What do you mean clean and change?" Trevor asked.

"It's not a big deal. I'll show you."

After helping Sissy lift Petey onto his bed, Trevor stood a full five feet away from the bed as he watched Sissy roll Petey on his side. Seeing an old person cleaned was gross. It was like watching a mother clean a hundred-pound baby. Trevor was glad when Sissy finished and they could lift Petey back into his wheelchair.

"Petey needs total care," Sissy said. "That means

he needs help with everything he does—dressing, eating, scratching his nose, cleaning, everything." Sissy glanced out the window. "It's a little chilly, so let's put a light jacket on him." She selected a blue jacket from the closet and pulled it on Petey backwards, tucking the zippers in along his side.

Sissy also took out a pair of sunglasses. "Use these if it's very sunny. Petey's eyes are sensitive after so many years inside." She picked up an old, worn photo album. "If you ever get the chance, these are pictures of Petey and some people he has known. He loves looking at them."

Trevor nodded but was silent as they rolled Petey outside. What had he gotten himself into? Taking his friend fishing was one thing, but no way would he ever clean and change Petey.

Sissy waved. "Have fun. Don't catch too many fish!"

Trevor began pushing, resting the fishing poles and worms alongside Petey's arms. Petey hummed as the breeze ruffled his fine, silvery hair. Several times Trevor stopped to make repairs. "I wonder if there is any way to get you a new wheelchair," he complained.

Petey shook his head sadly. "Oooo."

"We'll see," Trevor said. He stopped the wheel-chair and lifted his arms like a boxer after winning a fight. He pranced around Petey as he hummed the theme song from *Rocky*. Loudly, Trevor announced, "Hear ye! Hear ye! Trevor Ladd shall attempt the impossible! He shall get Petey Corbin one new wheelchair!"

Petey watched Trevor, amusement and puzzlement showing in his eyes as they continued.

After a half hour and several dozen "Ohh booees," they arrived at a small lake on the north end of Bozeman. Wheeling onto the dock, Trevor locked the wheels securely. He didn't want to take Petey swimming. Not yet.

Petey stared intently as a wiggling worm was threaded over a hook. Then Trevor positioned a bobber a yard up the line. "Petey, you're ready," Trevor said, casting the line out as far as he could. He tucked the rod snugly under Petey's limp arm and carefully rested the rod across his stomach so he could feel any movement. "Now, watch that bobber. If it goes under, tell me, okay?"

"Aeee, aeee."

While Petey eyed his line, Trevor fixed his own hook and cast it out. Trevor remembered how he used to fish with his parents. They didn't call it fishing—they called it drowning worms. But that was before Dad got his new job as a produce manager with a grocery store chain. Mom worked as an accountant. In fact, that was the whole reason they had moved to Bozeman—just so his parents could take better jobs. This was their third move in five years. Now they never did anything together anymore.

With two lines in the water, Trevor hoped a fish would bite on Petey's hook. Whenever a bobber wiggled, Petey's grunts came in short, excited gasps.

"Not yet," Trevor said. "When a bobber goes all the way under, then I'll jerk the pole and set the hook."

They watched the bobbers twitch. Suddenly Petey's bounced under. Trevor reached and gave the pole a sharp tug. Instantly the rod started jerking. Each tug sent surges of electric excitement into Petey's body, leaving him squealing and twisting in his chair.

Carefully, Trevor reeled in Petey's first fish, a six-inch spiny perch. He fought with it as if landing a gigantic whale. Glee filled Petey's face. Determined not to steal any of the fun, Trevor squeezed Petey's limp hand around the fish while he removed the hook. Sissy had said Petey had feeling in his skin even if he couldn't control his muscles.

Each time the fish wiggled, Petey thrashed his arms. Grinning, he kept up a constant barrage of "Ohh booee, ohh booee, ohh booee." When finally Trevor removed the hook, Petey looked at the little fish with a worried stare.

"What's wrong?"

"Oooo daa! Oooo daa!"

"Are you saying no die?"

"Aeee."

"Should I let the fish go so he doesn't die?"

"Aeee, aeee."

Trevor honored Petey's request, carefully letting the little fish splash free. They could have caught the Loch Ness monster and he would have still released it.

A short time later, Petey caught his second fish,

then his third and fourth. The fifth fish wiggled loose from Petey's hand, flopping wildly around on the wheelchair. Trevor thought Petey was going to hurt himself squealing and convulsing with delight.

That day, Petey caught seven fish. Trevor caught only one. The fish were only small rainbow trout or little spiny perch, but watching Petey catch them eclipsed any thrill Trevor had ever had fishing. Returning to the nursing home, Petey had fish slime all over his white cover sheet. He reeked of fish. Trevor was glad he hadn't needed to change Petey.

Sissy met them when they rolled in the door. She eyed the mess on Petey's sheet. "Well, it looks like you boys had fun."

Trevor and Petey both smiled mischievously.

As they said good-bye, Petey grunted at Trevor.

"What is it, Petey?"

"Shaaph."

"I don't understand. Is it something you want?"

"Aeee, shaaph."

"You're already wondering when we're going shopping?"

Petey grinned. "Aeee, aeee."

"What a slave driver!" Trevor faked exasperation. "Okay, is tomorrow soon enough?"

Petey smiled and nodded.

"You two are getting a regular social calendar," Sissy teased.

When he left Petey's room, he stopped Sissy in the hallway. "Hey, Sissy, is there some way to get Petey a new wheelchair? This one is falling apart."

Sissy frowned. "I doubt it. It takes an act of Congress to get any approval from the nursing home administrator. Doesn't hurt to ask, though. Bring Petey, let's try."

Together, Sissy and Trevor rolled Petey to the administrator's office. The short man, Mr. Hedrick, wore a freshly pressed suit. His hair looked glued in place.

After introductions, Sissy said, "Trevor, I'll let you explain to Mr. Hedrick the reason for our visit."

Nervously, Trevor reached down and pulled on the loose tire rubber. "Petey needs a new wheelchair," he said, showing Mr. Hedrick all the places he had used duct tape on the broken frame and upholstery. "Walking Petey with this chair is dangerous."

"Trevor," Mr. Hedrick replied politely, "the interest you have taken in this resident of *ours* is very nice. I understand this man's need for a wheelchair. We must, however, consider the limited benefit he might derive at such an advanced age."

It angered Trevor that Mr. Hedrick talked about Petey so indifferently, so technically. "Petey loves the outdoors," Trevor said strongly. "Without a new wheelchair to go outside, he probably *will* die." Trevor turned suddenly to Petey. "Hey, Petey. Do you plan on dying anytime soon?"

Trevor's question startled Mr. Hedrick, who blinked nervously, turning bright red. Petey laughed, whipping his arms around like stiff boomerangs. "Aaaa oooo daa."

Trevor pointed to a sign hanging over Mr. Hedrick's desk. It said, WE GIVE PEOPLE REASON TO LIVE, NOT TO DIE.

Mr. Hedrick dabbed at his hair as if the wind had ruffled it out of place. He stammered,

"Uh . . . no, it's not that simple. We need a physical therapist's recommendations. We'd also need pictures for Medicaid approval." Again the meticulous man shook his head deliberately. "Besides that, you would need *my* approval, which I will not give. This resident is too old to warrant that kind of expenditure. Can't you—"

Almost shouting, Trevor interrupted, "I hope *you're* in a busted-up wheelchair someday." Trevor grabbed Petey and pushed him out of the administrator's office. Immediately, he knew he shouldn't have said that. But somehow he would find a way to get Petey a new wheelchair. He didn't need the help of a lazy administrator!

Already Trevor had a plan.

Chapter 19

Before Trevor left that day, Sissy explained to him the process of getting a new wheelchair. "I can take the pictures," she said, "but Petey will need a physical therapist's evaluation. After that, you must work with a medical supply company. She paused. "Where will you get the money?"

"I have an idea," Trevor said excitedly. "But I need positive vibes!"

"Okay, here's positive vibes." Sissy wrinkled her nose, pursed her lips, and extended her long fingers toward Trevor like a sorceress. They both cracked up laughing. "Here's the phone number of one company in Billings and of a therapist who might help," she said.

Trevor left, giddy with excitement. Before his parents got home, he rode his bicycle to restaurants, asking them to save large coffee cans. After explaining his plan, most restaurants were glad to help. It was too late to make phone calls to the medical supply place, but tomorrow was Saturday. He would call then.

That night, Trevor told his parents all about Petey and about getting a new wheelchair.

"Is this okay with the nursing home?" Trevor's father asked.

"Yeah, they don't mind. Nobody there has time to take Petey for walks. This afternoon, I took him fishing," Trevor said. "He caught seven fish. I only caught one. Can you believe it? The guy is incredibly lucky."

Trevor's mother spoke up. "I'm a little concerned you aren't making friends your own age at school. Why are you getting so involved with this old man?"

Trevor wished he knew how to explain. The problem was, he didn't exactly understand it himself.

"You wouldn't understand," he mumbled.

"Try us," his dad said.

"Okay, I'll bring Petey by to meet you guys."

His parents exchanged glances as Trevor left.

Early the next morning Trevor got up and collected coffee cans in big plastic sacks tied to his bicycle handlebars. In a way, Trevor was glad to have the distraction of raising money for the wheelchair, because he hadn't made any real friends at his new school. Why should he? Every time he made new friends, his parents found better jobs and moved.

By late afternoon Trevor had collected nearly fifty cans. He had no idea how much a wheelchair cost, but it couldn't be more than a fancy bicycle, maybe two or three hundred dollars.

Next Trevor made phone calls. After the first one, his head was spinning. The medical supply company said that, depending on the modifications, a good wheelchair could cost over three thousand dollars!

"Three thousand dollars," Trevor groaned. "I can't come up with three thousand dollars." But already he had built up Petey's hope. Dialing one more number, Trevor tried to calm himself down. He needed to think straight.

"Hello, this is Georgia Adams," said a pleasant voice.

"Hi, are you a physical therapist?"

"Yes. May I help you?"

Trying to sound calm, Trevor explained why he had called.

"Do you have the funding for a wheelchair?"

"Not yet, but I—"

Georgia Adams interrupted, "If you don't have money yet, you're getting ahead of yourself."

Trevor took a deep breath. "I'll make you a deal. If I can come up with the money for a wheelchair, will you do the evaluation for free?"

She paused. "Okay, it's a deal. We need more people like you, who care."

"Thanks," Trevor said, hanging up. Having done all he could today, Trevor pedaled his bicycle to the nursing home. He still had time to take Petey shopping.

Petey's face beamed with anticipation as they walked to the store, but he seemed puzzled.

"Waa?" he kept asking.

"We're going to K-mart, Petey. That's a big store, where people buy things."

"Waaaee, waaaee?"

"Why do they buy things?"

"Aeee."

"Well, because they need things."

"Waa?"

Suddenly Trevor realized that Petey had no idea what shopping was. Was it possible that he had never been to a store in his entire life? "Petey, when we get there, I'll show you."

Petey nodded impatiently.

Soon Trevor rolled Petey across the K-mart parking lot. Out front, children rode bouncing animal machines while their parents deposited quarters. Petey stared at the children and the moving machines. "Ohh booee, ohh booee!" Staring, Petey puzzled. "Waa?"

Trevor balked. "Petey, they put money in the machines to make them bounce—it's fun for the children."

Petey still shook his head, confused.

As they entered the store, Petey's eyes darted

about. Bright, flashing lights, music in the air, children's screams, food smells—everything bombarded Petey at once. He squealed with delight. People turned and stared, not hiding their curiosity or disgust.

A tall, attractive woman walked toward them. Smiling, Petey flapped his bent arms. "Aaooo, aaooo," he called, his eyes filled with anticipation.

The lady regarded Petey without smiling.

Trevor spoke loudly as the woman walked past. "He said, 'Hello.'"

She ignored Trevor as well.

"Waaaee?" Petey asked, looking puzzled.

"Why didn't she say hello?"

"Aeee."

Trevor bit an angry lip. "Dad says beauty is only skin deep, but ugliness goes all the way to the bone!"

Petey laughed. "Ugggg!" he grunted. Then a stack of brightly colored boxes caught his eye. "Waa?" he asked, motioning with his chin.

"Those are boxes of pop."

"Ohh booee!" Petey's eyes darted to another object. "Waa?"

"That's a microwave oven."

"Waa?"

"It heats up food," Trevor added.

Petey looked puzzled.

"This must be like going to Disney World for you," Trevor said.

Petey looked up, still not understanding.

"Never mind, Petey. Compared to the nursing home, this must be incredible."

"Ohhh yaahhh, ohhh yaahhh!" Petey shouted, failing to notice the people staring, ducking down side aisles, or pretending not to see him as they passed. One set of parents regarded Petey fearfully and pulled their children to their sides. "Oooo guuu, oooo guuu," Petey said.

"No good," Trevor agreed. During their walk at K-mart, only two people smiled and said hello to Petey. Trevor wanted to hug them.

Petey insisted on knowing the name and purpose of hundreds of items. Trevor never realized how many objects were boxed with labels that someone like Petey could not read. Trevor felt like a bumbling fool. How was he supposed to describe how toy airplanes flew, how boats floated, how inner tubes worked, the purpose of tools and silly things like perfume?

Petey loved the perfume. He wanted to smell every sample. For some, he closed his eyes in bliss as if he were feeling the fragrance.

When they left K-mart it was getting late, but Trevor asked Petey, "Hey, would you like to meet my parents?"

"Ohhh yaahhh, ohhh yaahhh!" Petey exclaimed.

They stopped twice for repairs on the wheel-chair before making it to the house. Trevor parked Petey on the front lawn and went in to get his parents.

As his parents walked hesitantly from the front door toward Petey, Trevor saw in their eyes the same look of fear and disgust he had seen at K-mart.

Chapter 20

Trevor's parents smiled politely at Petey and spoke loudly in simple talk as if he were a deaf child.

"Just talk normally," Trevor said. "Petey can think, hear, and understand just like you."

Trevor's mom tilted her head toward Petey. "Oh, I'm sure he can," she said, speaking as if Petey wasn't even there.

"We gotta go," Trevor said suddenly, embarrassed by his parents.

"Well, thanks for stopping," Trevor's father said.

Trevor pushed Petey away from his house as fast as he could without knocking the rubber tire off the rim. "They treated you just like the people did at the store," Trevor blurted.

"Uuuuu," Petey grunted, motioning at Trevor.

Trevor felt embarrassed. "Yeah, I guess I did treat you like that to begin with. But that was before I got to know you."

Petey nodded his head patiently.

"Maybe people just need to know you."

Petey smiled. "Guuuu!" he grunted.

Trevor remained silent until they arrived back at the nursing home. "Do you want to go to your room or to the dining room?" he asked.

Petey jerked his chin and motioned toward his room. "Boooch!" he exclaimed.

Trevor wheeled Petey into his room. "Do you want to show me something?"

"Aeee. Boooch!"

"I'll bet I know what you want." Trevor took the photo album from the drawer.

Petey erupted with smiles and grunts. "Guuu, guuu."

Holding the album so Petey could see, Trevor

paged through the old photographs. Some were recent, taken at Bozeman Nursing Home. Others were old Polaroids taken back at Warm Springs. In one, a pudgy man sat smiling in a wheelchair, his thick glasses giving him cow's eyes.

"Ieeekk, Ieeekk," Petey exclaimed.

"Who?"

"Ieeekk."

"Was he a friend of yours?"

"Aeee."

"Where is he now?"

Petey's smile collapsed. He shook his head.

"You don't know?"

"Oooo."

Trevor continued paging through the pictures, while Petey looked on with pride in his eyes. Trevor realized that these pictures were the only bridge Petey had to his past, a past that was unimaginable. The people in this album were probably the closest thing to family Petey ever had.

Petey spotted another picture of the chubby man in a wheelchair. Jerking, he almost screamed, "Ieeekk!"

Trevor sat dumbfounded. The man had obviously been a very close friend of Petey's. "Maybe I can find out who he is," Trevor said. While Petey waited, Trevor took the album to some of the nurses. None had any clue as to who the mystery man might be. "Nobody knows him," Trevor reported to Petey.

Petey stared quietly at the photo album.

Sitting beside Petey, watching his eyes, Trevor could almost feel the ghosts of the past—a haunting past that begged not to be forgotten.

The next few weeks grew hectic with setting up the fund-raising for Petey's wheelchair. In every store that allowed it, Trevor placed a coffee can on the counter. He had cut a small coin hole in each top and taped a notice on the side explaining who Petey was and what he needed.

At the same time, school let out for the summer. Trevor had been at his new school a whole semester and still hadn't made any friends there. This gave him more time for walks. The spectacle of Trevor pushing Petey around town became a familiar sight. Slowly people overcame their fear and approached the odd couple to greet them.

By midsummer, Petey had met dozens and dozens of new people. Even some of the students from Trevor's school were stopping to say hello to Petey. Meanwhile, money for the wheelchair dribbled in—barely four hundred dollars had been raised. Petey's wheelchair broke down regularly. One day an axle broke. Trevor had to hold the chair up while a passing stranger called the nursing home for help. That day a local welding shop had to make repairs. It cost thirty-five dollars from the wheelchair fund. Now there was even less for the new chair.

"We'll never make enough for the new chair," Trevor complained to Sissy.

"Why don't you jump-start your fund drive?" she said.

"How?"

Sissy shrugged. "I don't know. Maybe contact the newspaper and have them do an article. There are people out there who might help if they only knew more about Petey and his life."

"I'll try," Trevor said. In minutes, he was out the door riding his bike toward the *Bozeman Daily Chronicle*.

To Trevor's surprise, the reporter at the paper seemed quite interested. She had noticed the fund-raising cans around town and had even seen Trevor out pushing Petey. She agreed to take a few pictures later in the week for an article in the Sunday paper.

"Thanks! Geez, thanks!" Trevor stammered as he left.

Pedaling as fast as he could, Trevor returned to the nursing home to tell Petey. Petey grinned with excitement.

"Let's go for a walk," Trevor said. "We'll go downtown and check the cans for money.

"Maaaaa," Petey echoed.

"Yeah, money." Soon Trevor was pushing Petey down a back street toward downtown. After only two blocks, the tire came off the rim again. When he stopped for repairs, Trevor noticed a frail old man hobbling toward them nearly a block away. The man carried a walking stick.

As Trevor finished wrapping tape around the rim and started to walk again, the old man called out, "Young man, please stop!"

Trevor turned. The man had his hand raised,

motioning for them to stop. "Is that you, Petey?" the old man gasped, breathing heavily from his pursuit. His wire-rimmed glasses hung crooked on his bony face.

Petey stared, recognition erasing his surprise. "Ooowwwee! Ooowwwee!"

"It is you, Petey. I can't believe it! After all these years!" the old man exclaimed.

"You know Petey?" Trevor asked incredulously.

"I should say so. I took care of him for many years at Warm Springs."

"Aeee, aeee." Petey's eyes filled with excitement.

The man extended his hand to Trevor. "I'm Owen Marsh."

"I'm Trevor Ladd, a friend of Petey's."

The old man shook hands forcefully, his grip stronger than seemed possible from such a thin and bony hand.

In less than a minute, a lazy afternoon's walk became magical as Owen explained how he worked on Petey's ward back in the sixties and seventies. The emotions between Owen and Petey left Trevor a little jealous. He had come to think of himself as Petey's best friend.

Owen, it turned out, was retired and living in Bozeman. Never once had he suspected Petey had been transferred from Warm Springs and lived nearby. Only two city blocks and a large open field separated his apartment building from the nursing home. It hadn't occurred to Trevor that for old people, a dirt field was as big an obstacle as any ocean or continent.

Before saying a reluctant good-bye, Owen gave Trevor his address and phone number. "You two visit me, okay?"

"Ohhh yaaaaa," Petey squealed.

"We'll visit," Trevor promised.

That night, Trevor lay awake. He had so many questions to ask Owen. How did Petey live at Warm Springs? Did they know he wasn't retarded? He thought about the photo album he had looked through with Petey nearly two months earlier. Would Owen know the chubby man in the wheelchair, the one Petey called Ieeekk? Finally Trevor slept. His dreams were filled with old men, photo albums, and new wheelchairs.

When Trevor woke, his parents had already left for work. Tired from not sleeping well, Trevor dragged himself from bed. Suddenly he thought of the photo album again and quickly pulled on his clothes. Without breakfast, he jumped on his bicycle and headed to the nursing home.

Petey was being fed breakfast when Trevor arrived. "Petey," Trevor asked excitedly, "does Owen know that guy in your photo album?"

"Aeee, aeee. Ieeekk, Ieeekk."

Trevor could feel Petey's excitement. "Okay, can I take your photo album over to show him?"

Petey jerked his head up and down. "Guuuu," he grunted.

Trevor pedaled his bicycle toward Owen's building, the album tucked in his belt. He hadn't called, but he hoped this unannounced visit was okay.

Owen answered his knock.

"I'm sorry for not calling first. Do you have a minute?" Trevor asked.

"I have all the time in the world," Owen said, grinning. "Everyone does, but they don't realize it till they get older. What's got you up and running like a jackrabbit?"

Trevor laid the photo album carefully on the table in front of Owen. "Petey has pictures of people he knew at Warm Springs, but he can't tell me their names. Do you know this one?" Trevor pointed to the chubby man in the wheelchair.

Owen stared at the picture, his eyes watering as he spoke. "Why, yes, that's Calvin Anders. I knew him very well. He grew up with Petey."

"Did you visit them after you left Warm Springs?"

Owen stared out the window. "I visited them once. After that visit, I heard Petey and Calvin had become severely depressed. So did I. Right or wrong, it hurt too much seeing them in Warm Springs, knowing I was powerless to help. Staying in touch would only have been a constant reminder and hurt everyone."

"Is Calvin still there?"

Owen's voice choked with emotion. "I've not seen Petey or Calvin since I visited them that once." He paused. "Although . . . I did see Calvin's picture in the Billings newspaper several years ago."

"The Billings newspaper?"

"Yeah, he was in the Special Olympics. I recognized him in a picture of the wheelchair race."

"Why isn't your picture in the photo album?" Trevor asked, immediately regretting his question.

Owen looked at Trevor, hurt by the implication. "This wasn't a vacation at Disney World," he said. "Not everyone got their picture taken with Mickey Mouse. To be honest with you, I never once saw a camera brought to the ward or thought of taking pictures."

"How retarded . . . uh . . . or handicapped is Calvin?" Trevor stammered, trying to patch up his blunder.

"Only slightly retarded, but he's severely clubfooted, which is why he's in a wheelchair. He was abandoned as a child during a snowstorm back in the 1930s. Over the years his muscles atrophied terribly."

"Whenever Petey sees Calvin's picture he keeps saying, 'Ieeekk.' That doesn't sound like Calvin," Trevor said.

Owen smiled sadly. "Ike . . . I never thought I'd

hear that name again. That's Petey's name for Calvin. He got it from an old Eisenhower documentary. It's a name he can pronounce."

Owen looked tired, so Trevor said, "Thanks, Owen, for all the information. Can I stop by again sometime?"

"Sure, anytime. And bring Petey with you. It's a little hard for me to get out and around these days."

After leaving, Trevor stopped back by the nursing home. "Hey, Petey," he said, finding Petey in his room. "That guy, Ike, was his real name Calvin Anders?"

Petey nearly choked. Flopping his arms, he squealed, "Aaeee! Aaeee!"

Trevor placed Petey's photo album back into the nightstand. "Maybe I can try to find Ike if you want."

Petey looked at Trevor doubtfully.

Once more Trevor raised his hands like a boxer and danced around Petey's wheelchair. Laughing, he announced, "Never fear when Trevor's here. If your friend is still alive, I'll find him!"

Petey did not smile.

As Trevor left, he wondered if he had made a second dumb promise he couldn't keep. He was still two and a half thousand dollars short for a wheelchair, and now he had promised Petey to find a phantom from a faded photograph. And even if he could find this guy, would he be getting old friends back together or was this digging up ghosts?

Chapter 21

Trevor did nothing to locate Petey's friend Ike. He wanted the idea to brew a while to make sure it wasn't a huge mistake. Meanwhile, the *Bozeman Daily Chronicle* arranged to do the article on Petey. Their reporter, Ann Turner, met Trevor at the nursing home, and for an hour asked questions and took pictures. She warmed up to Petey as they visited. That's how it always was when people met Petey, Trevor thought.

Trevor kept telling Miss Turner how badly Petey needed a new wheelchair. "I still have to raise two and a half thousand dollars," he repeated as she readied to leave.

"We're in the news business, not the fund-raising business," she answered. "But Petey really does have an interesting life story. Just think how different his life would have been if they had known what cerebral palsy was in 1920. . . ." She paused for a moment. "Petey is one of many people who didn't deserve to be put in an insane asylum. Sometimes certain stories touch hearts. I do hope this helps your friend."

"I do, too," Trevor said as she left.

Petey's face glowed, and his eyes danced with anticipation. After everybody had left and they were alone, Petey caught Trevor's attention. "Ieeekk?"

Trevor swallowed hard and looked at Petey's tired eyes. "Petey, are you sure you want to see Calvin again?"

"Aeee, aeee. Ieeekk! Ieeekk!" Petey grunted firmly.

"I figured so," Trevor said, "but I needed to be sure. Okay, I'll see if I can find him."

When Trevor returned home that afternoon, he picked up the telephone and placed a call to Warm Springs.

"Hello. Warm Springs State Hospital," a polite female voice answered.

"Hello, I need information about a past patient."

"Let me connect you with Records," the lady said.

A dozen rings later, Trevor heard, "Hello, Records. How may I help you?" The voice sounded impatient.

Trevor cleared his throat. "My name is Trevor Ladd. I need information about a patient that used to be at Warm Springs."

"Are you family?"

"No, not exactly. I just need to know where one of your patients is living now."

"Is it an emergency?"

Trevor hesitated. "No, I guess not."

The lady responded firmly. "I'm sorry, but you're asking for privileged information. Unless you're a relative, or unless authorized by the patient, that information is confidential."

"Ma'am, please help me. If I had authorization from the patient, I'd know where he lived and I wouldn't be calling you. I'm not asking for personal information, I just want to know where he lives."

"I'm sorry, but that *is* personal information."

Trevor gripped the phone with white knuckles. "Ma'am, what isn't personal, for Pete's sake? Can you even tell me what time it is, or is that privileged information, too?" He slammed the phone down.

As Trevor slowly relaxed his fists, he stewed. He knew he shouldn't get so mad, but he wasn't giving up yet. Hadn't Owen said something about seeing Calvin Anders in the Special Olympics? Trevor tracked down the Montana office for the Special Olympics and dialed the number.

"Hello. Special Olympics," answered a woman.

"Hello. My name is Trevor Ladd." Trevor decided that this time he'd take a more personal approach. "I'm close friends with a cerebral palsy patient named Petey Corbin."

"Oh, how nice, Trevor."

"Ma'am, I need some information. One of your participants is an older man named Calvin Anders. He and Petey grew up together in Warm Springs State Hospital. Both of them were abandoned there."

"How sad—can you imagine!" the lady said.

Trevor continued. "At Warm Springs, they were separated against their will." He took a deep breath. "Ma'am, can you please tell me where Calvin Anders lives so Petey can get ahold of him?"

"Oh, I'm sorry, Trevor, I'm not authorized to give out that information."

Trevor found himself again clutching the phone tightly. He tried to speak calmly. "All they had was each other. For years they were best friends until they were transferred out. Nobody cared if they were friends. Not until now. Ma'am, you're the only person I know who can help. Petey needs his friend. He's the closest thing to family he has. Please help me find Calvin Anders."

After an awkward silence, the lady said, "I'm afraid I can't tell you where he lives." Trevor was about to slam the phone down when she added, "But perhaps you could find him by calling group homes around the state." She paused. "Especially those in Hamilton. Do you want those numbers?"

Trevor stammered to find words. "Uh, yes. Yes, please! Thanks so much!"

"Oh, I didn't do anything, and *do* remember that."

"I will, but thanks anyway."

"You're welcome."

After five calls to Hamilton, Trevor flopped back on the couch with a groan. His parents would have kittens when they saw the phone bill. Determined to complete his mission, Trevor dialed the last number on his list.

"Hello," a dull, nasal voice answered.

"Hello, does Calvin live there?" Trevor asked.

The female voice giggled. "Nope, not here. This phone is in the kitchen, and Calvin's room is down the hall. If he lived here, he'd have to sleep on the stove. Then he'd get burned." Once more the dull, nasal voice cackled with laughter.

The woman's stupid humor left Trevor speechless. It took him a moment to realize he was talking to one of the residents at the group home. "That's not funny," he said.

Silence on the phone showed feelings had been hurt.

"Is Calvin in his room right now?"

"Nope, he's not around now."

Trevor figured he'd better make doubly sure Calvin lived there. "What's your name?" he asked.

"My name is Sadie," the lady announced proudly.

"Sadie, I'll bet you don't know Calvin's last name, do you?"

"Of course I know Calvin's last name. He lives here. . . ." She paused. "Not on the stove I don't mean. He lives down the hall." Again she cackled with laughter.

"So, Sadie, what's Calvin's last name?" Trevor asked.

"That's easy." Very slowly Sadie ground out the next sentence, playing with each word. "Hhiisss naaaammme iiisss Caaallvviiinnn . . . Aannnderrrsss. Calvin Anders!" she blurted. "Yup, that's his name. See, I told you I knew it." Once more she giggled.

Trevor tossed the receiver into the air and caught it. He'd found Calvin Anders! He was in Hamilton, a town nearly two hundred miles away. Trevor interrupted Sadie's laughter. "Thanks, Sadie, it sure has been fun talking to you. Remember, don't sleep on the stove." He could still hear her laughing when he hung up.

He shook his head and smiled. If people like her were really nuts, maybe the world needed a few more nuts. Immediately, Trevor called Sissy to tell her the news.

"I guess the next step is to call Calvin." Trevor said.

Sissy seemed hesitant. "Trevor, you better call the Social Services Director in Hamilton first and make sure getting together is something Calvin wants, too."

"Of course he would want to see Petey," Trevor said.

"You don't know that. I suspect Petey and Calvin have more history under their little finger-nails than you and I could haul in a truck. Make sure you're not stirring up a hornet's nest."

"Okay." Reluctantly, Trevor called the Social Service Director in Hamilton and explained the situation.

The lady seemed truly interested. "I'll talk to Calvin personally," she said. "If getting together is something that he wants, I'll let you know."

When Trevor hung up, his hands trembled. What if Calvin didn't want to get together? Then what? Trevor decided to avoid Petey for a couple of days. If Petey asked about Calvin, there would be no lying. Luckily, Trevor didn't have to wait long. The very next morning a call came from Hamilton.

"Hello," Trevor answered.

"Hello. I'm calling from the Hamilton Social Services Office. I have met with Calvin Anders and a volunteer advocate of his, Boyd Hanson. Yes, Calvin would love to see Petey. He was excited by the notion." The woman left the telephone number of Calvin's friend, Boyd Hanson.

"Yes!" Trevor screamed, hanging up. He boxed his fists at the air. Bursting with excitement, he rode his bike straight to the Bozeman Nursing Home. He couldn't wait to tell Petey.

Petey responded to the news with utter disbelief. "Ieeekk? Ieeekk?" His eyes blinked with surprise and a touch of fear.

Trevor didn't beat around the bush. He sat down and pulled Petey and his wheelchair alongside. "Okay, Petey, let's talk about seeing Ike."

"Guuu, guuu."

"Petey, right now I'm scared stiff."

"Waaaee?"

"'Cause I don't want anything to hurt you. You're happy right now, aren't you?"

Petey nodded.

"I'm afraid seeing Calvin will be like digging up ghosts. Maybe you'll remember things you don't want to. You're a lot older and smarter than me. There's not a single inch of you that's dumb. I know that, and you know that."

"Aeee."

"So, I'm not going to tell you what you can or can't do. You have to decide. Just think of the good and the bad that can happen."

Petey jerked his head up and down. "Aeee."

"Whatever you want, that's what we'll do."

For a split second Petey hesitated, as if afraid to hope for something that had been so painfully taken from him so long ago. Then all doubt disappeared with a broad smile. "Ohh yaaahh, ohh yaaahh!" Happy tears filled his eyes. "Thaaa uuu. Thaaa uuu," he grunted.

"You're welcome." Trevor bent over and

hugged Petey. "How did I ever get to like you so much?"

Petey grinned, and Trevor took a deep breath. It was time to dig up ghosts!

Chapter 22

Calvin's friend Boyd Hanson told Trevor he was surprised to find out about Petey. Calvin had mentioned him, but Boyd never dreamed the person really existed. Evidently Calvin fantasized a lot. "In three weeks, I'm visiting friends in Bozeman," Boyd said. "I'll bring Calvin along."

"Thanks," said Trevor.

After plans for the visit were completed, Trevor hung up the phone and took a deep breath. It was too late to stop anything now.

The long wait seemed almost cruel. For Petey, in

the tedium of the nursing home, three weeks became an eternity filled with way too much time to fret, worry, and build false hopes. Trevor didn't do well, either. Each night he tossed in bed, worrying about this powder keg he had pried open. What would happen when Petey and Calvin met after all these years apart?

To make the wait go faster, Trevor spent more time with Petey. He decided not to tell Owen or Calvin about each other ahead of time. There was no reason they should fret and worry unnecessarily.

Each day Trevor walked, fished, or checked the fund-raising cans with Petey. Donations had picked up following the article in the paper. Soon they counted over a thousand dollars. Still they were two thousand short.

One day, with rain pouring down outside, Trevor pushed Petey up and down the hallways of the nursing home. "I wish it wasn't raining," Trevor said. "We could have visited Owen today." As they passed the pay phone in the hall, Petey grunted and motioned with his eyes. Trevor stopped and looked at Petey, then at the pay phone. "You want to call Owen?"

With mischief showing in his eyes, Petey smiled and jerked his chin in a nod.

"Have you ever used a phone before?"

Petey shook his head and grinned. "Oooo."

Skeptically, Trevor backed Petey tightly against the pay phone so the receiver could reach his ear. As Trevor dialed Owen's number, Petey wiggled with anticipation.

"Hello," Owen answered.

"Hi, Owen, this is Trevor. I've got someone who wants to talk to you." He held the phone tightly to Petey's ear.

Petey's eyes grew wide. "Aaooo, aaooo!" he grunted.

Owen's side of the conversation couldn't be heard, but Petey's side made Trevor laugh. Petey talked to Owen for several minutes. Trevor knew when the conversation had ended. "Ohh, guuu baa, Owwweee. Guuu baa, guuu baa."

Trevor thanked Owen.

"You and Petey are good for each other," Owen said.

"Petey's good for everybody."

Petey sat smiling, completely enchanted by the new and magical experience.

To keep Petey occupied, Trevor asked him if he wanted to go to a movie.

"Aeee," Petey responded.

"What kind of movie would you like to see?"

Petey motioned toward his calendar. "Hooo."

Trevor saw horses on the calendar. "Something about horses?" he asked.

"Aeee," Petey said, nodding.

Trevor checked the movie listing. One movie, *Return from Snowy River*, had horses, so that night Trevor pushed Petey downtown to the movie theater. At the ticket booth he asked for one student and one senior citizen's pass. The ticket girl, who had long blonde hair and cute dimples, stared bluntly at Petey, ignoring his "Aaooo, aaooo."

Trevor recognized the girl from school, but he had never talked to her before. When her stare lasted beyond the normal curious glance, Trevor grew irritated. "Excuse me," he said, "do you need proof he's old?"

The girl shoved the tickets to Trevor, stammering, "Ah, no. No, that's not necessary."

As Trevor wheeled Petey into the show he was mad at himself. Without thinking, he'd gotten angry again and shot his mouth off. Now the girl was probably more scared of Petey than ever. When he found an empty aisle seat, Trevor set Petey's brakes and angled the wheelchair into the next row to avoid a runaway chair. Trevor waited until the show started, then he whispered to Petey, "I'll be right back."

Absorbed in the movie, Petey nodded in the dark.

Trevor tiptoed out to the ticket booth. The ticket girl sat counting receipts. Her long hair hung over one shoulder.

"Excuse me," Trevor said.

The girl glanced up and recognized Trevor, an uneasy look crossing her face. "Yes," she said, "may I help you?"

"I just wanted to say I'm sorry for getting mad."

The girl blushed. "Oh, that's okay, I deserved it."

Trevor grinned. "It still wasn't right of me to spout off like that. The guy is a friend of mine, and

I just want people to treat him normally."

The girl's face relaxed. "What's wrong with him?"

As Trevor explained, the girl grew more curious. "Can I meet him after the show?" she asked.

"Sure," Trevor said, surprised. "Petey would like that. By the way, my name is Trevor. What's yours?"

"I'm Shawna." She reached out and shook his hand.

"Well, I better get back to Petey."

"See ya after the show," Shawna called after him.

When Trevor sat down, Petey looked relieved, then returned his eyes to the screen.

The movie had great music, and Petey tried to hum along. The scenery kept him spellbound. All went well until the main character tried to kill a renegade stallion. When the fateful moment came and the man raised his rifle to aim it at the black stallion's head, Petey started shouting, "Oooo! Oooo! Oooo! Oooo!"

Every eye in the movie theater turned to look at Petey, then at Trevor. The man on the big screen

225

lowered the rifle as if obeying. Petey gave Trevor his best what-did-I-do look. Trevor squeezed his hand.

Later in the movie when the same character knelt tearfully beside a dying mare hurt during a bad fall, Petey again broke his silence. "Sooo saaahh, sooo saaahh," he wailed. Once more Petey had everyone's attention.

That night, Trevor realized he had quit being embarrassed around Petey. Wheeling him out of the theater, Trevor ignored the customary stares. As they passed the ticket booth, Trevor stopped. "I want you to meet someone," he said to Petey.

Shawna came around from behind the glass. "Hello, my name is Shawna," she said sincerely, looking down at Petey. "I'm glad to meet you."

Petey seemed confused. First he looked at Shawna and then at Trevor, puzzled over her sudden change in manners. When he saw Trevor smile, Petey returned Shawna's greeting. "Aaooo, aaooo."

"That's how Petey says hello," Trevor explained.

"I see you guys out walking all the time," Shawna said. "Can I come along sometime?"

"Sure," Trevor said.

"Aeee, aeee," Petey squealed.

The girl wrote down her name and number on a card and handed it to Trevor. "Promise you'll call me," she said.

Trevor couldn't believe this was happening. "Yeah, sure, I promise," he said.

As they left the theater, walking home in the dark, Trevor explained to Petey how he had apologized to Shawna for getting mad.

Petey nodded. "Guuu! Guuu!"

"It's hard not to get mad at people," Trevor said. "How come you don't get mad when people stare at you or treat you badly?"

Petey waited patiently for Trevor to answer his own question.

"Maybe people aren't really mean—it's just that they don't understand?"

Petey nodded and smiled gently. "Aeee," he squeaked.

"But how can you make people understand?" Trevor asked.

Petey looked into the darkness and shook his head.

Chapter 23

As Trevor counted down the days to Calvin's arrival, Petey grew more scared. Finally Trevor explained his plan. "Hey, Petey, tomorrow when Calvin gets here, let's hike up to Palisade Falls. The trail is paved for wheelchairs."

"Paaa Faaoo." Petey tried out the new words.

"Calvin's staying overnight, so Sunday morning we'll visit Owen. Remember, seeing each other is a surprise for both Calvin and Owen, okay?"

Petey nodded, his expression showing anticipation, fear, and excitement. All boredom had disappeared.

That night, Trevor did not sleep well. All night he tossed and turned, dreaming about two young boys laughing and running across an open field, chasing butterflies. All of a sudden the laughter faded, and the butterflies became wheelchairs. Trevor awoke in a cold sweat, breathing hard.

Saturday morning the dawn melted golden on the horizon as Trevor pedaled over to the nursing home. He wanted to get there early. Remembering how steep the trail became near the falls, Trevor brought along ropes to help pull the wheelchairs if needed. Sissy had arranged use of the nursing home van.

When Trevor arrived, Sissy had Petey up. "I have bad news," she said, greeting Trevor. "I need to work today. Two aides called in sick. You'll have to make your outing without me. Calvin's friend, Boyd, can drive the van."

"But it's too steep for me to push Petey up to the falls without help. Boyd will be helping Calvin."

"Shaaa! Shaaa!" Petey grunted

Sissy and Trevor looked at Petey.

"Shaaa!" Petey grunted again, looking at Trevor.

Trevor cracked a smile. "Are you saying Shawna?"

"Aeee!" Petey squealed.

"Who's Shawna?" Sissy asked.

"Just somebody we met," Trevor said. "She wanted to go walking with us sometime."

"Well, this would be a great time," Sissy said.

Not having any other choice, Trevor reluctantly called the girl they had met at the movie theater. Was she serious about going walking with Petey? He would find out.

"Hello," answered a cheery voice.

"Hi, this is Trevor Ladd."

"Hi, Trevor. I've been waiting for you to call."

"Listen, we're taking Petey up to Palisade Falls today with someone he hasn't seen in a long time. I was wondering if you wanted to come along. I could really use the help."

"It sounds fun. When are you going?"

"We're meeting this morning at ten o'clock in front of Bozeman Nursing Home."

"Sounds great. I'll be there."

Before Trevor could say thanks, she hung up. Trevor was sort of surprised. Maybe people weren't so bad after all. He put down the phone and turned to Petey. "Well, Petey, your girlfriend is coming."

Petey grinned and jutted his chin toward Trevor. "Uuuu," he grunted.

"Not my girlfriend," Trevor said. "No way!"

Before Calvin's arrival, Trevor helped lift Petey into the bath for a good scrubbing. Then as Sissy fed Petey, Trevor ran around getting everything ready: sack lunches, changing pads, towels and washcloths, van keys, extra shirts and sheets, and Petey's photo album to show to everyone. To finish preparations, Trevor covered Petey with a light blue sheet so he didn't look like he had come from a hospital.

As Trevor worked, Petey remained extra quiet.

"Is something bothering you?" Trevor asked.

Petey stared without answering.

Finally Trevor pushed Petey out onto the front lawn, and together they waited under a tree, eyeing each car that passed. "Ieeekk, Ieeekk," Petey grunted. At ten o'clock, Shawna arrived. While Trevor explained why the morning was so special, Petey kept watching traffic. Each time a new car approached, he held his breath. Finally a tan station wagon pulled slowly around the corner. The driver waved to them. "I think that's them, Petey," Trevor said.

Petey's eyes were riveted on the station wagon. As the vehicle stopped, a balding man with thick glasses was visible sitting in the passenger's seat.

Petey squeaked quietly, "Ieeekk, Ieeekk."

Trevor walked to the station wagon and introduced himself. Boyd Hanson shook his hand energetically, then pulled out a wheelchair and set it beside Calvin's door. "Do you want help with Calvin?" Trevor asked.

Boyd shook his head. "Calvin likes doing everything himself. He hates help."

For five minutes Calvin struggled to transfer himself from the car seat into his chair. He kept glancing over his shoulder at Petey and smiling. His smile exposed missing front teeth. Petey stared as if seeing a ghost. As they waited, Trevor told Boyd about the day's plans. Boyd agreed to drive the van up to Palisade Falls.

Completing the transfer, Calvin spun his chair around and wheeled toward Petey, his thin arms tugging desperately at the tires. Calvin was a short, rotund man. Though old, his toothless grin was that of a mischievous boy. "Petey, Petey!" he cried.

"Ieeekk, Ieeekk." Petey's eyes glistened.

Still several yards short, Calvin stopped and reached out. He couldn't yet touch Petey, so he bunched his cheeks and again maneuvered forward until he bumped Petey's chair roughly. He winced, then threw his body forward across Petey's bent knees and hugged. Petey sat quietly, allowing Calvin's actions to express his emotions as well.

Calvin looked up at Petey. "How ya doin'?" he asked.

"Pfer guuu. Uuuu?" Petey jutted out his chin.

"I been good, Petey. I thought you was dead!"

"Aeee, aeee."

Trevor stood beside Shawna, witnessing the reunion. He blinked back tears. Petey jabbered away in what sounded like gibberish. Calvin seemed to understand every sound as he smiled and held Petey's hand. "Petey, you ain't changed none. Remember this?" Calvin pointed his finger at Petey. "Ke, ke, ke."

Petey laughed, jerking his arms wildly in the air. "Kkkk, kkkk, kkkk."

Trevor stared in puzzled amazement. It was obvious the two old men were dancing in their memories.

"Look at us, Petey, we're kids again," Calvin said.

"Aeee, aeee, kkkk, kkkk." Once more Petey flung his arms out from his chair.

Calvin laughed, ducking so an arm wouldn't hit him.

"Petey, it's so good to see you. Did ya ever think you would see me again?"

"Oooo, oooo."

After several minutes their talking ebbed into silence. Calvin held Petey's arm against his chest, and they gazed at each other for a long while as all the world stood still.

Chapter 24

Early in the afternoon, the group arrived at the trailhead below Palisade Falls. "I'm so hungry, my big guts are eating my little guts!" Calvin announced.

"Then let's eat," said Trevor, laughing.

After eating their packed lunches, they began their expedition up the one-mile trail. While Boyd helped Calvin work his chair up the steep path, Trevor tried pushing Petey, then decided to use a rope. He tied one end around the frame. While Shawna pushed, Trevor pulled on the rope.

Twice they met other hikers who stared at their

strange convoy but greeted them warmly. Approaching the falls, Trevor hunkered down for the pull up the last steep section. Perhaps he pulled upward too hard, or Shawna pushed down. In any case, suddenly Petey's wheelchair tipped over backward.

With the chair resting on the hand grips, Shawna shouted, "Help me, Trevor!" Petey hung backwards, held in the wheelchair by Shawna's head and shoulder. Boyd couldn't help—he was holding Calvin on the steep incline. Trevor struggled to grab the frame. With a hard jerk, he tipped the wheelchair upright on top of himself. They began sliding down the path. Shawna dragged her feet while Trevor held on underneath for dear life, scraping along on his rear end. All the while, Petey laughed and squealed, "Ohh booee! Ohh booee!"

When they finally skidded to a stop, Trevor gasped with relief. Shawna broke into laughter. "You two are an accident waiting to happen!"

Trevor scrambled to his feet. "No way are we going to let a teeny little hill beat us, huh, Petey?"

"Aeee!" Petey squealed.

Boyd, who had reached the top with Calvin,

locked the brakes and returned to help. "Remind me to wear a helmet when I walk with you guys," he laughed, sweating.

Soon Petey rested beside Calvin near the falls. As everyone caught their breath, Petey studied the falls. "Hhoo?"

"How what?" Trevor asked.

"Hhoo, Paaa Faaoo?"

"How, Palisade Falls?"

"Aeee."

"Well, snow or rain drains into a river up above, and the river goes over a cliff."

Petey shook his head in disbelief, grunting something to Calvin.

"Petey says it's not winter and it's not raining, so that can't be." Calvin grinned, showing his missing teeth.

Trevor gave up explaining and turned to Calvin. "So how did you lose your front teeth?"

Calvin blushed. "I ran my wheelchair into a curb watching some pretty girls."

Everybody laughed. "You have to be careful around pretty girls," Shawna said.

"We're trying," Trevor said, winking at Petey.

On the footbridge, straddling the churning froth, everyone sat spellbound. The misty air breathed magic. Except for an occasional "Ohh booee, ohh booee," Petey and Calvin sat silently, lost in memories.

The sun had slipped low over the mountain peaks by the time the group worked their way back down the steep incline and returned to the van. Calvin dozed as they drove the winding road toward town, but Petey lay awake, a worried look creasing his forehead.

"What's wrong, Petey?" asked Trevor.

Petey refused to answer.

Little more than halfway to town, Trevor discovered what had bothered Petey. A foul odor filled the van. "Do you need changing?" Trevor asked.

Petey shook his head no.

Soon the smell became unbearable even with the windows open. "Petey, I'm sure you need changing," Trevor said.

Petey avoided Trevor's eyes.

Suddenly Trevor realized the reason for Petey's behavior. "Boyd, please stop the van," he said.

Boyd gladly pulled to a stop and everybody bailed out for fresh air. Petey stared at Trevor, then over at Shawna, concern wrinkling his forehead.

"Shawna, will you walk Calvin down the road a little ways until we're finished?" Trevor asked.

"Sure," said Shawna.

Boyd helped Trevor lift Petey from his wheelchair. They used the rear bed of the van for changing. "Have you ever done this before?" Boyd asked.

"It's no big deal. It's like changing a baby," Trevor said, not admitting he had never done that, either.

"How well do your parents know Petey?" Boyd asked.

Trevor chuckled. "They'd be having little batches of rabbits if they knew what I was doing right now."

"It's good learning to care for the elderly," said Boyd as they returned Petey to his wheelchair. "Someday, this will be us."

Finishing, Trevor pulled a clean sheet over Petey. "Petey, were you afraid Shawna would see you changed?"

"Aeee, aeee!" Petey exclaimed loudly.

"I'll never let that happen, okay?"

Again Petey nodded. "Thaaa uuu, thaaa uuu."

"All aboard!" Boyd shouted, and soon they were headed toward Bozeman. Calvin, Petey, and Trevor fell quickly into deep, relaxed sleep, exhausted by their adventure. They slept until the van pulled into Bozeman Nursing Home. Trevor woke with a start, realizing he had been leaning against Shawna. Embarrassed, he sat upright. Boyd looked back with a smile. "Did you all party last night?"

Petey and Calvin smiled mischievously.

"I better head home," said Shawna.

"Thanks for coming along," Trevor said.

Shawna flashed a smile. "Anytime. Good-bye everyone!"

After Shawna left, Trevor rolled Petey inside.

"Where will Calvin be staying?" Boyd asked.

"Uh, isn't he staying with you?" Trevor asked.

Boyd shook his head. "My friends have a small apartment. I thought this was something you had arranged."

"Maybe he can stay here," Trevor said, heading for the nursing desk. Soon he returned shaking his head. "They said Calvin can't stay here because there's no room and residents can't have guests."

"So what are you going to do?" Boyd asked, his voice making it clear this was Trevor's responsibility.

"He can stay at my place," Trevor said suddenly.

"Is that okay with your parents?" Boyd asked.

"We'll find out. It's easier to ask forgiveness than permission."

In five minutes they had unloaded Calvin beside Trevor's house. As Boyd drove off, Trevor's mom came out the front door. She stared at Calvin. "Trevor, what are you doing? Who is this?"

"This is Petey's friend I told you about."

"Why is he here?"

"Calvin is spending the night."

"Oh, honey, I know you mean well, but we can't keep him here."

Calvin's eyes clouded with fear. "Nobody wants me," he blurted.

"We have plenty of room!" Trevor said strongly, pushing Calvin past his mother and into the house. "I'll take care of everything!"

Trevor pulled couches together to make a double bed in the living room. His parents gave him accusing stares and made artificial conversation, then went to bed a full hour early. Trevor decided to start a fire in the fireplace.

Watching the flames, Calvin smiled broadly. "This is the nicest place I've ever been in my life." He leaned back against the cushions in bliss.

As the evening wore on, Calvin talked more. Each time he answered questions, he wrinkled his forehead and scratched his head. Sometimes he cradled his head in his hands, side to side. Clearing his throat loudly, Calvin voiced his opinion with an air of importance.

At times, Calvin spoke in a whisper as if telling secrets. He talked about a world unlike anything Trevor had ever imagined—a world of crazy people, walls, and screaming. He talked about Joe and Cassie and some of the people at Warm Springs who had been close to him and Petey. He told stories, some funny, some tragic. As he spoke, Calvin eyed a large black teddy bear resting beside Trevor on the couch. Trevor had won it years before at a carnival.

Without saying anything, Trevor picked the bear up and set it on Calvin's lap. Calvin pulled it in tightly, rubbing his cheek against the soft hair. "You know, Trevor, I always wanted a teddy bear. I saw pictures of them, but I never saw a real one."

"Well, would you like this one?"

Calvin blushed. "I'm too old now."

"I want you to have it."

A proud look crossed Calvin's face. He held the teddy bear at arm's length and examined it. "I'll take good care of it," he promised, hugging the furry toy to his chest.

"I know you will," Trevor said. He yawned and stood. "It's midnight, and I'm beat. Do you need help getting ready for bed?"

"No, I do things by myself. Just shut the lights out. I don't need light."

"Okay, good night."

"Good night."

Trevor went upstairs to his bedroom. For a long time he heard bumping and movement downstairs, but eventually he fell into a sound and welcome sleep.

Chapter 25

After staying up late, Trevor slept in. Finally, squinting at the bright sun flooding through the window, he rolled from bed and traipsed downstairs. His parents were still not up. Calvin lay curled on the couch, still asleep, hugging his knees like a child. The black teddy bear was tucked tightly under one arm. Contentment smoothed his face.

As Trevor read the comics section in the morning paper, he heard stirring and looked over to see a set of curious eyes watching him. He smiled. "Morning, Calvin."

"Morning, Trevor," said Calvin eagerly. He rubbed his eyes with his fists, like a baby.

"Did you sleep okay?"

"Yeah, but it was sure quiet." Calvin twisted his body so he could stare out the picture window. "I think I like quiet, Trevor. Yeah, I like quiet."

Remembering that Calvin prided himself on being self-sufficient, Trevor read without offering to help him get up. He stole glances above the page to see how things were going. Calvin threw back his covers and rolled onto his chubby stomach. Grunting and rocking, he slowly worked his way toward the edge of the couch with his thin arms. Each small advance was a victory of sheer determination. Finally, after some ten minutes, he sat himself upright on the edge.

As Trevor moved on to the sports section, he tried to watch the living room without being noticed. His caution proved unnecessary. Calvin lay on his stomach again, struggling back across the couch to where he had forgotten his brown jumpsuit. Another five minutes and he had the jumpsuit securely clenched in his teeth, dragging it slowly back to the edge. Soon he rested again on the edge of the couch, breathing heavily, his jump-suit in hand.

Trevor stood and took some food outside to feed the cat. Calvin was so engrossed with dressing that he didn't notice Trevor return to the kitchen. He had the jumpsuit pulled over his twisted feet and bunched around his waist. Lying back on the couch, he flopped from side to side like a stranded fish, yanking at the fabric, working it up his body. With each pull, he grimaced.

Trevor wanted so badly to walk down and help. A full hour had passed since Calvin had begun getting up. Another five minutes passed before he could coax his zipper all the way up. He sat a moment, mustering strength for the swing into the wheelchair. Beads of sweat glistened on his forehead. He closed his eyes, tilting his head backward to face the ceiling.

Then, with a mighty heave and a grunt, Calvin swung out into midair. He hung for a split second between the couch and wheelchair, then with a muffled thump he landed heavily on the leather seat. A broad grin spread across his face as he looked up and caught Trevor staring. "I do this every morning," he said. "I do good, don't I?"

Trevor couldn't believe what he had just seen. The simple act of dressing had been a monumental achievement. Trevor felt like running around the room, singing, clapping, and jumping up and down in celebration. All he could stammer was a clumsy "You bet. I mean, yeah, you did great!"

Calvin grinned at Trevor. "I sure got it easier than Petey."

Trevor shook his head in admiration as he went upstairs to call Owen Marsh. He needed to see if Owen minded a visit.

"Hey, Owen. Can Petey and I visit you this morning?" Trevor asked nervously. He spoke quietly so Calvin wouldn't hear.

"Of course," Owen said cheerfully. "I'm always glad to see you two."

As Trevor hung up, he wondered if surprising Calvin and Owen was the right thing to do. Trying to ignore his worries, he helped push Calvin toward the nursing home.

"Hey, Trevor," Calvin chirped. "Boyd says that a jewel is just a rock that figured out how to shine."

"Well, that's interesting," Trevor said, being polite.

Calvin's face wrinkled in thought as he peered back at Trevor through his thick glasses. "That's what Petey and I are—rocks."

"Rocks?" Trevor asked.

"Yeah, we just don't shine."

Trevor stared at Calvin. What other thoughts like this were in that head that was supposed to be retarded?

Calvin waited for an answer.

"I think you do shine, Calvin," Trevor said.

"You really think so?" Calvin's astonishment exposed the gaping hole left by his missing teeth.

"Yup, I really think so."

Calvin shook his head as he rolled along. "I never thought I was very special before."

When they reached the nursing home, Boyd hadn't arrived yet, so Trevor left Calvin on the first floor and went upstairs to find Petey. He discovered him in the dining room where a service was being held by volunteers from a local church.

Residents sat grouped around tables, most of them unaware of the program. Off-key music pounded from an old upright piano. Some residents slept, their snores mixing with the broken singing. Some stared off into space, unresponsive to the volunteers' cheerful questions: "Are you happy?" "Isn't this a wonderful day?"

Trevor glanced around and found Petey near the window, staring serenely out at the sky. Petey was the only person in the room who seemed totally at peace with himself. "Good morning, Petey," Trevor whispered, tiptoeing up beside him.

"Aaooo, aaooo," Petey grunted loudly with a smile. Several heads turned to investigate the intrusion, glaring disapproval. Quietly, Trevor rolled Petey from the room.

Outside the door Trevor said hello to Murphy, one of the residents. The old retired rancher stood inspecting the church service through a lobby window. His crippled body bore no resemblance to the young strapping man in the old family picture on his bedstand downstairs. Murphy reminded Trevor of an old thistle bush. Now Murphy wallowed in well-earned cynicism. "You guys are the only smart ones," he growled.

"What do you mean?" Trevor asked.

"You're leaving." Murphy motioned back toward the church service. "That noise makes my ears hurt!"

"Aeee, aeee," Petey chimed in.

Trevor wasn't about to argue with these two wise and grizzled survivors of time. He pulled Petey into the elevator and pushed the first floor button.

Downstairs, they found Calvin introducing himself to everyone. Puffing his chest up with importance, Calvin announced over and over, "I'm Petey's friend." Trevor smiled as he rolled Petey to his room to get ready.

Just as Trevor finished, Boyd showed up and they were off on their walk to Owen's apartment. Calvin grew more excited with each mention of the person they planned to surprise. He didn't like the suspense. Nor did Trevor anymore. At least a dozen times Calvin pleaded, "Come on, Trevor, who is it? Please tell me?" Petey squealed with excitement and secrecy.

When they reached Owen's apartment, everybody remained on the lawn while Trevor went inside and knocked on Owen's door.

"Well, how are the caped crusaders today?" Owen asked cheerfully. His bushy hair was freshly combed, and he moved lightly on his feet. Trevor noticed the bounce in Owen's step. Was it really possible that Owen was almost ninety? Only his gnarled hands truly showed his age.

"Where is Petey?" Owen asked.

"He's downstairs on the lawn. We have somebody else for you to meet."

"Now who would that be?" Owen asked.

"You'll see," Trevor said, trying to keep his voice from shaking.

Owen walked out the door onto the lawn, squinting toward the visitors. Calvin stared back with a puzzled stare. Then as Owen came closer, Calvin cocked his head to one side, recognition flooding his eyes. "Owen! Owen!" he screamed. "Is it you?"

Owen stopped in stunned disbelief. His voice shook. "Boy, Trevor, you sure stirred the kettle this time." He walked over and kneeled in front of Calvin. He placed a hand on Calvin's shoulder. "Hello, Calvin," he said.

"Owen, what are you doing here?" Calvin asked.

"I live here. You're sure looking good."

Calvin blushed. "I do?"

"Yes, you do."

Calvin's smile faded. "Owen, how come you didn't keep visiting us like you said you would?"

Owen did not rush his answer. "Sometimes when something hurts too much, you can't do it, no matter what you've promised."

"Did it hurt visiting us?"

"It hurt seeing you in Warm Springs and not being able to help you. Do you remember how sad you were after my one visit?"

Calvin nodded his head. "Why didn't you adopt us?"

Big tears swelled in Owen's eyes, and he bit his lip. "I was seventy-three years old. I couldn't take care of you."

"I wouldn't be no trouble," Calvin insisted.

"I know you wouldn't. I was just too old."

Petey listened intently, his eyes glassy.

Trevor stood fidgeting. "Owen," he said, "I can't believe Warm Springs separated these two, knowing they had been friends all their lives."

Owen spoke patiently. "It wasn't their fault. They had to relocate several thousand patients. They returned most to their original counties. Calvin needed a group-home setting. Petey needed total care. Even if they had wanted to, these two couldn't have stayed together. It was the right decision."

Trevor shook his head. "At least they could have sent them to the same town!"

Petey sat quietly, listening to every word. When the talking lapsed, Petey seized the opportunity. He flapped his arm over the side of his wheelchair and looked over at Calvin. Bunching up his cheeks, he sounded, "Kkkk, kkkk, kkkk."

Calvin broke into cackling laughter. Lifting his arm, he turned and pointed his index finger at Petey. "Ke, ke, ke."

Owen joined the laughter.

"They did that when they first met yesterday, Owen," Trevor said. "What in the world are they doing?"

"These two haven't changed one bit. Someone gave them toy pistols when they were young. I guess they used to have some pretty lively shoot-outs on the ward. It took me about two years to figure out what they were up to myself. An old nurse remembered seeing them with the pistols, and explained their actions to me."

Owen turned. "Trevor, it's good what you did today. Life has never been fair to these two, and they've never asked for anything more than what they had. Today I reckon you gave back to them both friendship and hope. That's a lot."

After a long visit, Owen and Calvin said reluctant good-byes, promising to visit again soon. On the way home, Trevor and Boyd started their own shooting game with Petey and Calvin. Before long, all four were dodging and ducking the make-believe bullets. Petey, it turned out, was invincible. He was the only one who never died. Calvin on the other hand, went through death throes perfected during years of battle. Before he expired, his head flopped to one side, tongue protruding. A loud, mournful wail pierced the air, ending with guttural coughs and a couple of spastic jerks.

After reaching the nursing home, Calvin and

Boyd said their good-byes. Petey watched until their car disappeared, then made it clear he wanted to go inside. When Trevor rolled him into his room, Petey motioned with his chin toward the closet and grunted.

"Is there something in your closet that you want?" Trevor asked. Petey nodded and motioned toward the top shelf. Trevor dragged down a dust-covered cardboard box. Piece by piece he pulled out old clothes, broken sunglasses, an old horse calendar, a busted transistor radio, several nearly empty bottles of shampoo, a dirty blue handbag, and two old hats.

Then Trevor caught his breath. In the bottom of the box lay a toy pistol and a holster. Trevor picked up the pistol and rolled it over in his hands. The silver paint was chipped and worn.

Chapter 26

Calvin's visit lowered Petey gently into melancholy. His summer, so filled with new experiences, had been the most enjoyable of his entire life. Events brought life full circle, satisfying his need to touch the past.

As autumn neared, donations for Petey's wheelchair slowed to a trickle. Most business owners were wanting the big coffee cans off their counters. Reluctantly, Trevor tallied the final count: two thousand nine dollars. How could he tell Petey they had come up short? All summer he had promised, "We're almost there, Petey. Just a few more dollars." But a thousand dollars was more than a *few*!

Frustrated, Trevor asked Sissy, "How much does the company make that is selling the wheelchair?"

Sissy shrugged. "Maybe twenty or thirty percent."

"Like maybe a thousand dollars?"

"Could be, why?"

"Money has quit coming in, and I'm still a thousand dollars short for Petey's wheelchair. I think the company should give Petey his chair without making any money."

"But that's their business," Sissy said.

"Do you have any better ideas?" Trevor asked.

Sissy shrugged. "I guess not."

Not daring to face Petey, Trevor rode his bicycle home. He called the company in Billings and asked to speak to the manager.

"Hello. May I help you?" answered a man's businesslike voice.

"Yeah, hello. My name is Trevor Ladd." Trevor breathed deeply. "I've been trying all summer to raise three thousand dollars to buy a wheelchair. All I can come up with is two thousand." Trevor paused awkwardly. "So would you sell me the wheelchair for two thousand?"

"I remember you calling several months ago. You were interested in a chair specially fitted for an elderly resident with cerebral palsy, wasn't it?"

"Yeah, he's my friend. I know it's a lot to ask, but will you sell it for two thousand?"

Now the awkward silence came from the man. "I'm sorry, at that price the company wouldn't make a dime."

"But Petey is special!" Trevor blurted.

The man coughed nervously. "In our business, every case is tragic and special. We—"

"Not like Petey," Trevor interrupted, scrambling for ideas. "The newspaper did an article, and everybody in Bozeman knows about Petey. If you give him the chair for two thousand dollars, I'll tell everybody what you did. Maybe the newspaper will do another article."

"I suppose I could allow a small discount."

"It has to be a thousand." Trevor pleaded. "I've tried my hardest and don't know what else to do. Please help Petey."

"Well . . ." The man's voice softened. "If you can

provide me with an evaluation from a physical therapist, I'll see what we can come up with."

Trevor shouted, "Thanks, thanks a billion!"

"No, just thank me a thousand," the man chuckled. "I think Petey has himself a very good—and persistent—friend."

After hanging up, Trevor called the physical therapist. He wondered if she still remembered their deal. She did.

Trevor whooped at the top of his voice as he hung up. In seconds he was pedaling his bicycle like a maniac toward the nursing home to share the news with Petey.

For Trevor, school had begun again. Often Shawna joined him and Petey on their daily walks around town. Sometimes she even took Petey out alone if Trevor was busy. One afternoon when they showed up on a rainy day, Petey looked at Trevor and Shawna and said, "Gooo fiii."

"You want to go fishing in the rain?" Trevor asked.

Petey shook his head and jutted his chin toward them.

"Gooo fiii!" he said forcefully.

"But we can't fish when it's raining," Trevor said.

Petey shook his head in frustration.

Shawna spoke hesitantly. "I think he's telling us to go have fun."

"Aeee, aeee!" Petey squealed, nodding.

"Are you telling us to go have fun?" Trevor asked.

A kind and gentle smile filled Petey's face. "Aeee."

Trevor and Shawna gave Petey hugs before leaving.

After Petey's wheelchair was ordered, time dragged by. Trevor wondered if the company had been serious. But finally, one week before Halloween, the new wheelchair arrived. Trevor examined the machine he'd worked so hard to buy. It was finally here! He couldn't believe it was real: the shiny chrome, the heavy-duty frame, the brand-new tires. "Has Petey seen it yet?" he asked.

"Not yet," Sissy replied.

Excitedly, Trevor rolled the new chair to Petey's room. Petey stared, his gaze sweeping over each precious inch of the shiny, deluxe model. "Guuu," he grunted.

Trevor crawled into the new wheelchair, his legs braced straight out, and spun it in circles. After a couple of tries, he did a wheely, almost tipping over.

Petey laughed, flapping his arms.

"Okay, it's your turn," Trevor said.

With Sissy's help, Trevor placed fresh pads and a sheet over the chair. It took some adjustment, but soon Petey settled comfortably into his new home. His "Guuu, guuu, guuu" could be heard clear down the hallway.

"Petey," Trevor exclaimed, "now that you have a new wheelchair, let's do something special for Halloween."

"Waa?" Petey asked.

"I don't know, I'll think up something special."

Good to his word, on Halloween Trevor celebrated by dressing Petey up as Batman. He dressed himself as Robin. With cardboard and paint, Petey's wheelchair became the Batmobile. Shawna wanted to be a part of the celebration, so she dressed up as the villain Joker.

Petey glowed. This was more than a Batmobile.

This was his mount, his magnificent stallion, his greatest physical possession.

Soon Christmas arrived. When Trevor stopped by to drop off Petey's present, he didn't need a calendar to know it was Christmas morning. Dozens of cars jammed the visitors' parking area. The rest of the year that area stood vacant.

Trevor had bought Petey a framed plaque with a Bible verse on it about rising up on wings like eagles, running and not being weary. His own family didn't even go to church, but the plaque had seemed like something nice.

When they opened the present, Petey gestured and made it clear he'd heard the verse before. Try as he might, however, he couldn't communicate the circumstances. Trevor did figure out that it was back in Warm Springs. Several times that day, Petey asked Trevor to read the plaque again. Each time they reached the part that said, 'they shall mount up with wings like eagles,' Petey stopped him. "Peeshhons," he blurted.

Trevor never did figure out what 'peeshhons' meant.

One day in January, several boys asked Trevor if he wanted to play basketball after school.

"I have to visit Petey first," Trevor said.

"Hey, can we see where Petey lives?" one boy asked.

Trevor hesitated, then shrugged. "Sure, if you want."

Together they walked to the nursing home and into Petey's room. Trevor saw in his classmates' eyes the feelings he had first felt entering this building.

Petey grunted, "Aooo, aooo," at each boy.

They nodded and said hello back.

"Waaa?" Petey said, motioning toward the boys.

"Why are they with me?" Trevor asked.

Petey nodded.

"They wanted to see where you lived."

"Guuu," Petey grunted.

"So, what do you want to do today?"

Petey jutted his chin toward Trevor and the other boys. "Gooo fiii."

"You want to go fish?"

263

Petey shook his head. "Uuuu gooo fiii!" he grunted.

Trevor remembered Petey doing this same thing to him and Shawna. "Are you telling me to go play with these guys?" Trevor asked.

"Aeee," Petey grunted, a smile smoothing his face.

"Okay, but I'll come see you later."

"Gooo fiii," Petey repeated.

"Thanks!" Trevor called back as he left.

In late February, Petey came down with a fever. Each day he grew hotter. At night he tossed and turned restlessly.

One night, at two o'clock in the morning, Sissy made her rounds. Trying not to wake Petey, she rolled him over and wiped him clean in the darkened room. Sliding a clean pad under him, she folded the dirty one and deposited it in the laundry. She failed to notice the dark bloodstains.

In the morning when she snapped on the light to wake him, she found Petey twisting on the bed, his eyes pinched closed, his face twisted in pain.

Sissy ran to his side. "Petey, what's wrong?"

Petey choked, vomit surrounding his head.

"Oh, my God, Petey, what's wrong? What's wrong?" A foul smell hung in the air. Sissy pulled back his cover, staring at his bloody pad. "Jamie! Bill!" she screamed. "Come quick! Something's terribly wrong with Petey!"

Within fifteen minutes an ambulance was wailing its siren as it raced across town.

Chapter 27

At the hospital, a young anesthesiologist changed slowly out of his scrub clothes, glad his shift was over. It had been a very long night. Several auto accidents had him bone weary and ready to go home.

As he picked up his jacket, a voice called down the hall, "Dr. Waters, hold up a minute. We may need you."

Dr. Waters shook his head. "What now?"

"We've got a guy coming from Bozeman Nursing Home."

Dr. Waters groaned his frustration.

The patient turned out to be a twisted and elderly cerebral palsy resident named Petey Corbin. He had a severe bleeding ulcer in addition to pneumonia. The surgeon, Dr. Cross, decided quickly not to operate. The patient had incredible deformities, was over seventy, had no family, and was in very poor health. Guttural grunting also brought into question his mental state. Dr. Cross doubted the quality of life that would exist even if they could save him.

"Dr. Waters, go on home. We're better off leaving this one alone," Dr. Cross said.

Dr. Waters sighed with relief and headed out the door.

Word was sent to the nursing home that Petey would be kept heavily medicated to make his final hours easier.

Several hours later when Dr. Cross made his rounds, he checked in on Petey. As he entered the room, he stopped. More than a dozen people stood crowded around the old patient's bed, sobbing or blinking back tears. Flowers covered the nightstand and window sill.

"What's going on?" demanded Dr. Cross. He

was certain this patient had no family.

A roomful of tear-soaked eyes turned accusingly toward him. A young high-school boy wiped at his freckled cheeks and stepped forward. "I'm Trevor Ladd. We heard that you weren't going to operate. Why not?"

"Young man, our decision was based on the quality of life this patient could expect." Dr. Cross did little to hide his irritation. "Someone this age, in this state, with no family, should be allowed to die with dignity."

Petey gave the doctor a piercing stare. "Aaaa oooo daa, aaaa oooo daa," he coughed.

"And what about *his* wishes?" Trevor asked.

"What wishes are those?"

"He just told you, 'I no die.' You just didn't understand him. As for family, he's got us."

Dr. Cross stared dumbfounded at the patient, at the freckled boy, and at the group of pleading eyes. He coughed sharply. "I'll reexamine the lab results, but don't get your hopes up."

"Our hope is already up," said Trevor.

Soon Dr. Cross reentered the room, the air thick with anticipation. "We'll operate," he said quietly.

A burst of claps and cheers irritated Dr. Cross. Already the schedule was full. Now he would need to call Dr. Waters back for anesthesia.

Bleary eyed, Dr. Waters returned. He tried asking Petey questions. Lack of communication made his patient analysis difficult. He had no idea what brought the change of plans, but he questioned the surgery.

Wheeling Petey into the operating room, Dr. Waters noticed his unmistakable look of fear. "Don't worry, Mr. Corbin, you're in good hands," he said, stopping the gurney. He rested his hand on Petey's shoulder and looked directly into the old man's eyes. "Is this operation something you want?"

Petey's nod, little more than a blink of his eyes, was unmistakable.

Nurses lifted Petey onto the operating table, gawking at the contracted legs across his stomach. Petey's gaze raced around the large, cold room, inspecting each masked person. A nurse hung up his intravenous tube. Cold patches made Petey jump as they were placed on his shoulders and chest. Deftly Dr. Waters attached leads to a heart monitor.

When they wrapped a blood pressure cuff on his arm, worry creased Petey's face. After positioning a small ear clip to measure oxygen in the blood and placing another patch on Petey's arm to measure muscle relaxation, Dr. Waters held a mask firmly over Petey's face. Petey's anxious look became a chilling stare.

Uneasy silence blanketed the operating room. Eyes met above faceless surgical masks, exchanging glances of reproach. Dr. Cross resented the unspoken blame and air of absurdity surrounding this medical effort. He approached the table, holding his freshly scrubbed hands in the air. He scanned the balled-up mass of human flesh lying before him, then shook his head. "How soon are we ready?" he asked. "This patient will be a handful."

"Soon," said Dr. Waters as Petey fell asleep.

Late that evening, Trevor was allowed to see Petey for the first time after his operation. A catheter tube snaked out from under Petey's blanket, and an IV bottle dangled over his head. Petey shivered with fever. Trevor rested his hand on Petey's forehead. He had never seen anybody this sick. Petey opened his eyes briefly, too weak to move.

"How are you?" Trevor whispered.

Petey did not respond.

Each day when Trevor visited, Petey's fever grew worse. His hacking cough turned to ragged choking; his face became gaunt and drawn. What scared Trevor the most was Petey's hollow eyes. Instead of seventy, he looked one hundred.

The sixth night, the nurse met Trevor at the door to Petey's room. "Petey's pneumonia hasn't responded to medication," she said. "Now he has rigors."

"What's that?"

"Uncontrolled chills and fever. Several times his fever has hit one hundred six," she answered.

"Can I still visit him?"

"Sure. He may be asleep. He's had a rough day."

As Trevor entered the room, Petey opened his eyes a fraction of an inch—enough to show his fear. Sweat beaded on his forehead, and his face had become ashen.

"How are you?" Trevor asked.

An uncontrolled spasm of shivers forced Petey's eyes closed. His grimace answered Trevor's question.

"Are you afraid of dying?" Trevor blurted.

Petey opened his eyes. "Waaaee?" His weak voice almost gasped the word.

"Why? I don't know. Some people are afraid of dying. I just wondered if you are."

Trevor could barely hear Petey whisper, "Oooo," as his eyes closed.

"I better go and let you sleep."

Petey cracked open his eyelids again and strained to move his hand against Trevor's. "Oooo," he grunted.

"You want me to stay?"

Petey nodded by tightening the muscle in his chin.

It made Trevor happy that Petey wanted him there. They sat maybe two hours in silence, holding hands. Trevor wondered what dreams Petey had. Quietly, not sure Petey even heard, he said, "Petey, if there's another life after this one, I'll bet we see each other again. You'll have a brand-new body that can climb big mountains. You'll speak normally and say anything you want, and people will understand you."

A thin and peaceful smile tugged at the corners

of Petey's mouth. Trevor continued. "I'll chase you, but I won't be able to catch you."

Petey opened his eyes weakly. "Waaaee?" he whispered.

"Because you'll run faster than the wind. You'll be shouting and screaming like crazy."

Trevor had to watch Petey's cracked and dried lips to understand his "Guuu." Petey's face relaxed.

"Just one catch—if there is another world, you're gonna have to put my worms on the hook when we go fishing."

Petey could make no more sound. Trevor rested his hand on Petey's chest, feeling the labored breathing. Petey had fallen into a stuporous sleep. Trevor looked at the clock and winced. It was after ten. His parents would be going nuts. During the past week, the hospital had become his second home.

As Trevor left, he stopped by the nurses' station. "Excuse me, can you do me a favor?" he asked.

The nurse wrote as she spoke. "What's that?"

"If Petey gets worse, can you call me? I don't care if it's the middle of the night, I want to be here." He paused. "Can you call Sissy Michael, too?"

"Are you family?" she asked, looking up.

Trevor thought. "We're the only family he has."

The nurse wrote down the information. "We'll call you and Sissy if his condition changes," she said. "Right now, it's not looking good. His fever won't break."

"If Petey asks for me, he makes the sound 'Twaaa.'"

"Twaaa," the nurse said, jotting it down.

As Trevor rode his bicycle home through the dark, the highway kept blurring. He blinked. Feelings ripped at him, leaving big, open wounds too deep for words. When he reached home, his parents met him at the door. "I don't want you out at this hour," his mother said firmly.

"But Petey's in the hospital!"

"Your mother is right," his father agreed. "Petey has professionals taking care of him. You don't need to get so involved."

"He's my best friend!" Trevor said firmly, keeping his anger in control. His parents just didn't understand, he told himself. Deliberately he went to his bedroom. Not until that moment did he realize how much he needed Petey. Last year he had never even heard of this wonderful old man. Last year, Trevor knew, he himself hadn't understood. Petey had given him the creeps.

Trevor lay awake, unable to sleep. He asked questions in his mind, the kind without answers. He didn't remember falling asleep, but the loud, shrill ringing of the phone jarred him rudely awake. His mind panicked as he fumbled for the receiver beside his bed.

"Hello," he stammered.

"Hello, is this Trevor Ladd?"

"Yeah."

"This is Bozeman Hospital. Can you come in?"

"I'll be right there," Trevor said, hanging up the phone. Frantically he dressed. As he ran out the front door, he saw lights blink on in his parents' bedroom. Trevor didn't care anymore—Petey was dying. In seconds, he was pedaling his bicycle down Bozeman's dark and deserted streets toward the edge of town.

As he rode, he wished things could have been different. He wished that Petey could have known a family. And he wished that he could have been part of it. Sure, Petey had great friends, but all Petey's friends eventually left him. Nobody was really family.

It was too late for anything now, Trevor thought, noticing the light gray of dawn that tinted the horizon. A spring chinook wind blew wet mist against his face as he pedaled into the hospital's lighted parking lot. He dumped his bike on the grass and ran inside, not noticing his parents' car pulling into the lot behind him. Trevor bounded up two flights of stairs.

On Petey's floor, something had happened. Nurses scurried about, grabbing equipment and hollering orders. A nurse pushing a cart from Petey's room told Trevor, "Go on in." Trevor rushed in and found Petey lying motionless. Sissy Michael was already there, standing quietly beside the bed. Holding his breath, Trevor tiptoed to the bedside and looked down. "Is he okay?"

Sissy shook her head.

Petey stirred and his eyes opened. "Petey, I'm here," Trevor said, his voice trembling. "I . . . I want you to know that I'm here." He couldn't

276

make out Petey's expression in the dim light. Nor did he see his parents step quietly inside the darkened doorway. They stood watching.

Trevor stared at Petey. "Can you understand me?"

"Gooo fiii," Petey grunted weakly.

"You want to go fish?" Trevor asked incredulously.

With great effort, Petey shook his head. "Uuuu gooo fiii."

Trevor took a deep breath. "Are you telling me to go have fun without you?"

A thin smile creased Petey's face.

"I'll try, Petey." Trevor said. Petey had taught him so much, especially how to have fun and appreciate life. Could he go on without him?

"Can I ask you something?" Trevor blurted.

When Petey did not respond, Trevor asked, "Will you be my grandfather?"

Petey looked puzzled.

"You don't have a family, and neither do I . . . not really. I don't have any brothers or sisters. My grandparents are dead, and my parents always work."

Petey mouthed the word, "Aaooww?"

"Petey, family isn't something on paper, it's something in here." Trevor touched his chest. "Family is different than friends. You'd always be my grandfather in my heart. You'd be stuck with me—I'll never leave you."

Petey didn't smile. He probed Trevor's eyes for any crack or flaw of intention. "Ggg faaa," he said faintly.

"Yeah, grandfather."

Petey's eyes warmed, and an intense and haunting smile filled his face. "Ggg faaa," he repeated.

"And I'd be your grandson."

"Aeee, aeee." A gentle stare relaxed Petey's face as the joy and wonderfulness of the notion sank into his thoughts.

There were no words for the moment. Trevor leaned forward and wrapped his arms around Petey, resting his head on Petey's chest. With his cheek he could feel a heartbeat, a ceaseless rhythm that had existed since the beginning of the century.

Sissy reached out and laid Petey's limp arm across Trevor's neck. Trevor wondered if anyone else had ever felt the weight of Petey's arm like this. Trevor's parents watched from the shadows in hurt silence. His mother dabbed at her eyes.

Slowly Petey relaxed, his body borne away into slumber by emotions he'd never known before.

Trevor released Petey and looked up. A soft sunrise was unfolding outside Petey's window. "Is Petey dying?" he whispered.

Sissy paused. "We're all dying from the second we're born. That's why it is so important to live."

"That's why Petey told me to go fish, isn't it?" Trevor said. "He meant that I should go live my life now without needing him."

Sissy smiled tearfully. "We'll always need Petey. But you're right. Petey may die tonight . . . or next week. Trevor, you have your whole life ahead of you. Petey's life has been about living. If we can learn this one thing from Petey, his life will have counted for something *very*, *very* important."

Trevor stared at Petey, then at Sissy. Blinking back tears, he forced a smile. "Then let's go fish."

Sissy gave Trevor a big hug. "Let's go fish," she said.

As he finished hugging Sissy, Trevor noticed his parents standing inside the doorway. "How long have you guys been here?" he whispered.

"Long enough to know we haven't been the family we should be," his father said.

"It's no big deal," Trevor choked. Awkwardly, Trevor's father glanced at Petey. "It is a big deal. I guess we just didn't understand. You've made us see that caring should be everybody's business."

Trevor's mother spoke. "It's time for us to stay in one place and make roots. It's time to be a family again."

Trevor studied his parents. "You really mean that?"

His father nodded. "Like Petey said, it's time to go fish." He motioned toward the door. "Let's talk outside so we don't wake him up."

Reluctantly, Trevor followed everybody from the room. In the doorway, he stopped and looked back. He whispered, "I'm going fishing, Grandpa Petey." He spoke the words slowly and with respect, tasting each word as it came off his tongue.

The words tasted good.